BEWARE!!
DO NOT READ THIS
BOOK FROM
BEGINNING TO END!

ARE YOU READY FOR *ANOTHER* NIGHT IN TERROR TOWER?

"We're not from your time," your friends Sue and Eddie tell you. "We're really a prince and princess—from eight hundred years in the past!"

Yeah, right, you think. But before you know it, Sue and Eddie have dragged you back in time. And then they get captured by their enemy, the Executioner!

Now it's up to *you* to rescue your friends—and find a way back to your own time. But can you handle a dragon? Cast a spell? Match wits with Robin Hood?

And can you beat the evil Executioner?

This story picks up where GOOSEBUMPS #27, *A Night in Terror Tower*, left off. But this scary adventure is all about *you*. You decide what will happen next!

Start on Page 1. Follow the instructions at the bottom of each page. If you make the right choices, you'll find your friends again. But if you choose badly . . . BEWARE!

NOW TURN TO PAGE 1—TO *GIVE YOURSELF GOOSEBUMPS!*

READER BEWARE —
YOU CHOOSE THE SCARE!

Look for more
GIVE YOURSELF GOOSEBUMPS adventures
from R.L. STINE:

R.L. STINE

GIVE YOURSELF

Goosebumps®

SPECIAL EDITION #2
THE NIGHTMARE CONTINUES:

RETURN TO TERROR TOWER

AN
APPLE
PAPERBACK

SCHOLASTIC INC.
New York Toronto London Auckland Sydney

A PARACHUTE PRESS BOOK

ISBN 0-590-39999-3

12 11 10 9 8 7 6 5 4 3 2 1   8 9/9 0 1 2 3/0

Printed in the U.S.A.   40

First Scholastic printing, May 1998

"The Lord High *who*?"

You stare at your friends Eddie and Sue Morgan.

Sue scowls.

"The Lord High Executioner," she repeats. "We told you about him already. Are you even listening?"

"I'm listening, I'm listening," you answer. "But this story is a little hard to keep up with."

You munch another cookie and take a swig of milk. The truth is, you *aren't* really listening. The three of you just got out of school. It's a warm spring day. There's a breeze blowing. Now that you've had a snack in the Morgans' kitchen, you want to go outside and ride your bike, maybe have an adventure. If that's even possible in your rinky-dink little town.

But Sue and Eddie insist on telling this crazy story first. About how they're actually a prince and princess from medieval England.

Yeah, you think. And I'm the president of the United States.

Turn to PAGE 2.

2

Sue pushes a lock of blond hair out of her eyes and keeps talking. "Over eight hundred years ago our father was the king of England. Like I said, I was Princess Susannah, and Eddie was Prince Edward. Our father was a good king. He treated his subjects kindly. Eddie and I were to step into Father's place as rulers of England."

"Sue, Eddie! Reality check! Your father is Professor Morgan," you interrupt. "He teaches history at the university."

"He's not our real father," Eddie says.

"Where's your real father, then?"

"He's dead," Eddie replies. You see a cold, hard look in his eyes. "He was murdered by our uncle. After that, Uncle Robert had himself made king. He used magic to turn the nobles against us."

"And he had help," Sue adds with the same hard look. "From the world's most cruel, evil man — the Lord High Executioner."

Find out more on PAGE 3.

"The Lord High Executioner?" you repeat. A chill races up your spine.

"He's a twisted, evil man," Eddie declares. "He loves to inflict pain and suffering. After Uncle Robert became king, the Executioner locked us in the Tower. It's a terrible place — full of instruments of torture. We were being kept there until the Executioner could burn us at the stake."

Eddie shivers and goes silent. Sue picks up the story.

"Our father's wizard, Morgred, rescued us. He sent us to this time, your time. We were in London. But the Executioner followed us. He kidnapped us and took us back to the past. And he almost killed us again. Morgred saved us for the second time. He brought us to this time again. And we moved all the way to the United States. Now Morgred stays with us and pretends he's our father."

When she finishes, there's silence in the room. It's a crazy story. And you're beginning to think that Eddie and Sue believe it! Does that mean your friends are crazy?

Maybe you should get out of here. There's still plenty of time to go for a bike ride.

Or maybe you should stay with your friends.

If you hit the open road, turn to PAGE 53.

If you hang out with Eddie and Sue, turn to PAGE 105.

"Getting rid of the king is more important than getting me back to my time," you declare, trying to sound brave.

"I knew you'd say that," Sue tells you proudly. "Okay. Listen up. We know King Robert is using magic to make the nobles and the guards and soldiers follow him."

"It sure isn't his personality," you joke.

Sue and Eddie grin.

Then Eddie's face gets serious.

"The problem is, we don't know how he does it," he tells you.

But you might know! Did you have a little chat with his ghostly lordship?

If Lord Worcester told you the source of King Robert's power, turn to PAGE 106.

If you didn't talk to Worcester, turn to PAGE 30.

The wagon pulls into the marketplace. Peasants and nobles line the streets to stare at you. Most look away nervously. But one slender figure in a green hood and cape stands in the lane and looks you straight in the eye.

"Hey! I know that person," you whisper to your friends. "It's —"

Suddenly loud battle yells come from the trees surrounding the market. Then dozens of green-cloaked men and women jump from the branches and into the square. They begin to battle the startled soldiers.

In one smooth move, Robin whips off her cape and leaps onto your wagon. She knocks the driver into the mud and cracks a whip over the horses' backs.

The wagon bounces into high speed as the startled horses gallop wildly through the market.

Suddenly, you see five burly men wearing red-and-black tunics. They're blocking the road out of the market!

Turn to PAGE 16.

The soldier squints at you down his crossbow sight. A dozen other armored men stand behind him with gleaming swords.

"Halt!" another voice cries. The voice is so strange and cold, it seems to cut you to the bone. A tall figure in a black cape steps forward. His face is shaded by the hood of his cloak.

"Do not harm this one," the evil voice commands.

"Yes, Lord High Executioner," the knight answers.

The Lord High Executioner? Your heart sinks at the name. This is the man Eddie and Sue fear more than anyone.

The Executioner leans way over in his saddle. With a dagger, he spears the soccer ball. It collapses limply.

"Did I not tell you, Captain?" he gloats, waving the ball. "The enemies have strange things. Like this work of evil."

The soccer ball! That's how they spotted you.

The Executioner tosses the limp ball to the dirt.

"Take this one to the Tower. Then the real games can begin."

He laughs. The sound turns your blood to ice.

Oh, well. Eddie and Sue told you you'd have to go to the Tower. Problem is, you won't be sneaking in. You'll be going though the front door. And for you, that means

THE END.

You glance at the waiting boy. "Sorry," you say, "but she's right. I'd better hide."

The boy looks disappointed. He shrugs and walks away. You turn to the girl.

"Where are the soldiers?" you ask.

"Everywhere," she says. "They come at all times, taking our food, demanding more and more. It hardly pays to work the fields anymore. And we're all hungry."

A look at the girl's gaunt face shows you she's telling the truth. You begin to realize why Eddie and Sue had to come back.

"But why don't the people rebel?" you ask.

The girl grimaces. "The king's spies are everywhere. If anyone says anything, they haul 'em off to the cursed Tower. Once that Executioner gets his hands on you, you're good as dead." She lowers her voice. "Me own father was taken away last year. We never heard from him since."

"I'd better get out of here," you mutter. "Where —"

But you don't get a chance to finish. At that moment you hear rough voices nearby and the sound of a chain-mailed fist banging on a door. The girl's face freezes with fear.

"Quick, hide!" she hisses. "They're searching the village!"

Hide on PAGE 131.

"But where is here?" you cry.

Sue's lonely voice comes to you through the fog. "Nowhere."

Lost forever? In this weird, frightening nowhere place? You've been holding it in. Now you scream with all your might.

But all you hear is a thin cry coming out of your own mouth. From what seems like far away, a few voices cry back.

"Help!" screams one.

"Someone get me out of here!" calls another, faintly.

After a while, you get used to being nowhere. And that's a good thing. Because you're going to be there until

THE END . . . OF TIME.

The spells at the front of the book are probably for beginners, you think. I'll start with one of those.

You open the book and peer at the first page. Once again, the letters seem to swirl and shift. Then you can read them.

BEGINNER'S SPELL, it says at the top of the page.

"Just what I thought," you say to yourself. You read on.

> *This spell is for real beginners. It's a good place to start. In fact, it's where everybody starts. Just say it three times.*

If this is where everybody starts, how dangerous could it be? you think.

You take a deep breath and read aloud the words printed at the bottom of the page:

"Anthroporum! Shnorum-Torum! Paleozoic! Leeuwenhoek!"

You read them aloud again. And then a third time.

Nothing happens.

I guess I did something wrong, you think, feeling a little relieved. Then in the next breath, the room vanishes in a flash of blue light.

Travel to PAGE 37.

You walk toward the Executioner — even though that's the last thing you want to do!

He's got you in some kind of trance.

As you get closer, the Executioner studies your sunglasses.

"Ah," he gloats. "Ray-Bans. I saw those when I visited the future.

"Unfortunately, sunglasses won't help you," he continues. "I may not be able to see your eyes, but you can still see mine. Pretty gnarly, eh?"

You feel yourself locked in his gaze again. Your willpower is totally gone. In another moment you will be completely under his control. He will force you to tell him everything you know about the stones and Eddie and Sue. You've failed.

Your mind is slipping away.

But at least you look cool!

THE END

"Sorry, there must be some mistake," you say as politely as you can. "I just . . ." You were about to say "took a wrong turn," but you never get the chance.

The tall man grabs you by the hair. "Talk back, will ye?" he growls. "I'll teach ye to talk back to me!"

The next thing you know, he's dragging you out of the castle and down to the market. He pulls you over to two boards mounted on a post.

"Into the stocks with ye," he snaps. He pushes your head and both hands onto one board with hollowed-out spaces. Then he slaps the other board on top so that the boards hold your head and hands tightly.

A large crowd quickly gathers.

"This child needs to be taught a lesson in obedience!" the tall man shouts to the crowd. "Go ahead. Do your best!"

The throng steps forward eagerly. Several people bend down and scoop up rocks. The men and women wear cruel grins. A huge bear of a man lifts his fist, which holds a large rock.

"No!" you scream. But you can't move. You can only watch in horror as the man hurls the heavy stone straight toward you.

Go to PAGE 90.

The swords poke into your chest.

You suck in your breath. And hear a harsh metallic *CLANG*. Then another, and another.

You open your eyes — to see the last of the guardsmen drop their swords to the stone floor.

"I'm free!" one guardsman shouts.

"It's a miracle!" shouts a noblewoman in a feathered hat.

Soon the whole Throne Room is echoing with the shouts of men and women who have been released from Robert's spell.

You look over at Robert. He has fallen to his knees.

"No!" he shouts, raising his fist and shaking it. "Noooo!"

The crowd rushes forward and lifts Eddie and Sue onto their shoulders.

"Long live the true prince and princess!" they chant as they parade your friends around the room.

Meanwhile, others have grabbed Robert, who had started to slink away.

Then the doors to the Throne Room are flung open. The cheering dies, and Eddie and Sue are gently set down.

Filling the doorway is the Lord High Executioner.

Turn to PAGE 110.

"But, Sue. I mean, Susannah. I mean, Your Princess-hood," you stammer. "It's time for me to go home, isn't it?"

"But you are home," Eddie says, grinning.

"No, I'm not!" you protest. "My home is —"

You stop. Somehow you can't remember your home. Or your parents. Or your school. Or anything from your time.

"What's wrong with me?" you murmur. "Am I under a spell?"

"No," Sue says gently. "You *were* under a spell. The same spell that Morgred put us under when he hid us in the future. A spell to make us forget who we really are."

"Who we really . . ." You trail off. "I'm not from the future?"

"No!" Eddie cries. "You are from this time. You're our cousin! This castle is your home too!"

You can't believe it. You *don't* believe it. But suddenly all your memories come flooding back. Eddie and Sue are telling the truth. You really are one of them. This really is your home.

Your royal cousins hug you.

"You did it!" Eddie says. "You restored us to the throne. And now we can rule, together!"

You take a deep breath. You set out to help a royal family. How could you know that you'd be helping yourself?

Congratulations. And long live you!

THE END

It must be a trick. Holding tightly to the key in your pocket, you back away from the nobleman. There's another door leading from the room. You back toward it.

"You fool!" Worcester cries. "Stop!"

Frightened, you yank open the door and jump through without looking. There's no floor on the other side! Suddenly you're falling. You cry out in pain as you strike rough rock walls on your way down. With a jolt you strike a cold, hard, rock floor.

After a long moment, you dare to open your eyes. Worcester is standing next to you.

"You fool!" he says again. "You should have trusted me. Now you're lost, and there's nothing I can do for you. Edward and Susannah should have picked more wisely."

"Edward and Susannah?" you murmur.

Then Lord Worcester vanishes into thin air!

You stagger to your feet. You're in a cave carved into solid stone. A thin beam of light comes down the shaft you fell through. You stumble about, searching for Worcester.

"Where did he go?" you wonder out loud.

"Where did who go?" someone answers.

See who said that on PAGE 100.

It's just too chancy. If you spend any time with this nobleman, he's sure to see that you're not from old England. But how do you say no to a rich, powerful aristocrat?

"Uh, sorry, sir," you begin. "But my mother expects, uh, expecteth me home for supper."

The rich man's smiling face clouds over immediately.

"You little wretch!" he roars. "You dare to defy the Earl of Worcester? I'll teach you not to be so proud!"

He draws his sword and raises it as if to strike you on the head. You turn around to run. You feel the hiss of air as the blade whips by your left ear, narrowly missing it.

When you look up, you see that you're in the middle of the drawbridge, facing the castle gate. The guards heard the nobleman's shouts and they're running toward you!

Behind you the earl is stepping closer, his sword point aimed for your heart. You're caught!

Or are you?

Without giving yourself time to think, you run to the edge of the drawbridge. The water in the moat below is black and murky. And you don't even know how deep it is. But what choice do you have? As the nobleman raises his sword for another swipe at you, you take a deep breath and jump.

Hit the water on PAGE 38.

16

"Watch out!" you cry to Robin.

"I see them," she calls back.

Standing on the wagon seat, Robin cracks the whip in the air again. "Yah!" she screams to the horses.

The wagon bounces even faster. At the last minute, the soldiers jump out of the speeding wagon's way. They tumble into the manure-filled ditches lining the road.

Soon the wagon is bouncing through an open field.

"Sorry we're late!" Robin calls back to you.

"That's okay!" You laugh as the wind whips through your hair.

"Thank you for the rescue," Eddie shouts. "But where are you taking us?"

Find out on PAGE 67.

Your two friends leap to their feet and rush to embrace you.

"You found us!" Eddie cries.

"I knew you would!" Sue adds.

As quickly as you can, you fill them in on your adventures.

"But we don't have time to talk," you say after a minute. "We have to get out of here."

"Yes," Sue agrees. "Before the Executioner discovers us."

"But first we have to get back our stone," Eddie adds. "The Lord High Executioner took the one we kept."

"No," Sue objects. "There's something more important. First we have to find a way to get Uncle Robert off the throne. We have to find the way to break his power."

Eddie touches your shoulder. "You decide."

You pause at the entrance to the room. You feel torn. Part of you just wants to get back to your own time. The other part feels that Sue is right.

But how can King Robert be overthrown? You think back on your adventures so far. Is there something you've learned that will help you?

Decide what to do now.

If you go after the missing stone, turn to PAGE 46.

If you try to overthrow King Robert, go to PAGE 4.

In a loud, clear voice you shout out, "K-M-P-E-P-C-B!"

Then, for good measure, you add, "Plus two!"

The sound echoes. But nothing happens.

I might as well give up, you think, feeling tired. You lean against the wet pink wall next to the door.

Wet pink wall?!

You jump back in fright. That wall was cold white stone just a second ago. Now it's soft and wet and pink, like, like . . .

Like the inside of a mouth! With a terrible feeling, you turn and see that the jagged gray stones around the entrance are now white shiny fangs. The entrance is now a giant mouth, and the jaws are closing! The floor under you has turned into a giant pink tongue — and the doorway is opening into a dark throat!

You turn to run, but the sharp teeth snap shut.

The doorway *is* magic, but the letters were the wrong thing to say. Some other word must open the door, but you'll never find out now. The huge molars around you begin to gnash and grind. The giant tongue is heaving and pushing you around.

You lose your balance and fall over one of the teeth. You look up to see its partner coming down, straight at you.

Just before the crunch, you can't help but think that the teeth are snowy white.

This tower must brush after every meal!

THE END

Standing next to you is a cloaked figure who seems to have appeared out of nowhere. You jump back, in fright, still shaky from your narrow escape.

"Who are *you*?" you ask, your voice quivering.

"A friend," the cloaked figure murmurs.

"I don't know if I need any more friends," you reply.

The stranger laughs. "A wise point of view. But it's not safe to be wandering in this forest alone."

You relax a little. Even though you can't see this guy's face, you don't feel threatened.

"Why don't you follow me?" the stranger suggests. "If you see anything you don't like, you can always stop. But I think you'll do better with me than with them."

You look down the road. The men chasing you were scared off by something, and it wasn't you. Could they have been scared by this person — who isn't much taller than you?

"Okay," you say. "I'll go with you."

"Good," replies the stranger. He steps off the road through some dense bushes. If there's a trail, you don't see it.

"Where are we going?" you ask, pushing through the bushes.

"To Robin's camp," comes the answer.

Go to PAGE 78.

"Had you killed?" You repeat the words dumbly. It's all you can do to keep from keeling over.

Is this guy a ghost?

"Yes!" Worcester replies, his voice rising in anger. "By the Lord High Executioner, because I dared to oppose Robert's grab for the throne. It was many years ago. But my spirit has never left this castle. I use my ghostly powers to appear alive to King Robert and the others. They don't remember who I *really* am. I cannot leave until Robert is defeated and the rightful heirs are restored to the throne."

He points a thin finger at you. It looks pale and almost transparent. Worcester is fading in front of your eyes!

He leads you to a heavy wooden door, which swings open. On the other side is blazing daylight.

"This path will lead you back to the crossroads," the spirit tells you. "Now go! Avenge me!"

You turn to thank him, but where he stood is only thin air. Shuddering with fear, you run out into the warm sunshine. Then you head down the path to the crossroads.

Turn to PAGE 32.

"What do you mean?" you protest. "Of course I'm going."

Sue shakes her head. "No. It was wrong of us to bring you here. But you have been brave. And you've been victorious. Now Edward and I must regain our throne by ourselves."

"No!" you shout. "I want to stay! I want to help you!"

"We won't put you in any more danger," Sue replies.

"Sue! Please!" you beg. She ignores you.

"Eddie?"

He smiles sadly at you as he piles up the stones. Then he chants, "Movarum, Lovaris, Movarus!"

CRACK! You're blinded by a flash of blue light.

The next thing you know, you're standing in Eddie and Sue's house. You touch the kitchen table — it's real.

"I'm back!" you whisper to yourself. "I'm in my own time!"

You jump in the air and shout, "Yahoo!"

Then you sink into a chair. The whole experience has been mind-blowing. And you realize that your friends Eddie and Sue are still in danger. They still have to fight their uncle.

You know you could have done more for them. If only you could get a second chance.

A second chance . . .

Can you get a second chance?

THE END

The secret passage leads to a maze of tunnels. Some are so small you have to crawl through them. You try not to think about how far underground you must be.

Eddie and Sue seem to know the way. You scramble after them, bumping your head on sharp rocks. Finally, the three of you crawl out of the last tunnel. And stand up in a small room.

"We're right behind the Throne Room," Sue whispers to you, pointing to a large wooden panel. She uncovers a peephole in the middle of the panel. You press your eye to it.

And almost cry out in fear!

The king's throne is only a foot away. And beyond that is the vast Throne Room, crowded with people.

"If we study Robert, we might learn the secret of his power," Eddie whispers, kneeling down next to you and Sue. "We think it's some magic object. Maybe his scepter."

"Just be careful," Sue warns you. "Don't lean on the —"

With a loud crack, the panel you're leaning on splits in two. You and the panel and Eddie and Sue all tumble forward — right into the throne!

Bang into PAGE 102.

You decide to try the climb again.

Finally, by pressing your feet against one side of the shaft and your back against the other, you manage to inch your way up. It takes all your strength, and once or twice you almost fall, but finally you reach the top and climb out into bright sunlight.

You lie there panting until you catch your breath and your eyes get used to the light. Then you pick yourself up.

Grimly you remind yourself that you still have to rescue Eddie and Sue before you can get home. It's time to get moving again.

Glancing around, you recognize a big, pointy rock that you saw on your way in. You start walking. Soon you find yourself back at the crossroads.

Turn to PAGE 136 and write: Magic Stone. Then turn to PAGE 32.

It might be risky, but this may be your only chance to get into the castle. You take a deep breath.

"Yea, um, v-v-verily, My Lord," you stammer, trying to remember how they talk in movies. "I wouldeth be much honored."

The nobleman grins. "Follow me, then," he commands.

You walk behind him as he crosses the drawbridge. The guards on both sides bow to him. They don't give you a second look.

Wow! you think as you try not to step on your new master's embroidered velvet cape. That was easy!

As you enter the main courtyard of the castle, you don't know where to look first. There's even more to see here than at the market. The palace guards lounge around, polishing their swords with dirty rags. Servants rush back and forth with bags and baskets. You stop to stare at a company of knights clattering by on their chargers.

"Come along," your master urges. "We mustn't keep King Robert waiting."

"King Robert?" you repeat.

Your heart begins to pound. If the king finds out who you are, he'll send you to the Tower!

Meet the king on PAGE 132.

Slowly, almost painfully, the dragon ra.... from the pile of jewels. It's more terrifying... you could have imagined. It's part dinosaur, p.... nightmare. Its back, legs, and wings are covered with thick, sharp spines, each one taller than you.

You're too scared to run. You stand frozen.

The dragon's long neck snaps out with terrifying speed. Its huge mouth is only inches away. You almost faint from the smoke pouring out of its mouth. You fall to your knees, trembling, ready for the end.

"There is but one thing that will save you," the dragon breathes in an eerie whisper. "More treasure for my hoard. What have you brought me?"

Treasure? You rack your brain, trying to think of what you can give the dragon for its treasure trove. What do you have in your book bag?

If you brought your flashlight, go to PAGE 49.
If you brought your tape player, go to PAGE 63.
If you brought both, choose PAGE 49 or PAGE 63.

"I have an idea," you whisper. "Can you find the table in the dark?"

"I think so," Eddie whispers back.

"Good, then get ready."

You brace yourself, trembling. In spite of your fear, you have to force yourself to do this. It's your only hope.

You dart from the stairwell and into the arched stone chamber. The Executioner reacts quickly, more quickly than you'd planned. He turns and raises his thin hand.

"You!" he says in a voice that almost stops your heart. "Come here."

You try to avoid his gaze, but you feel your eyes being drawn to his. Your feet slow down, almost by themselves. You struggle toward the table, keeping your eyes lowered.

"Look at me!" he commands.

Almost helplessly, you raise your head and — blow out the candle on the table! The room is plunged into darkness. Immediately you hear the sound of feet scuffling on the stones behind you.

A second later you hear Eddie's voice.

"I have the stone!"

Turn to PAGE 88.

Even if this woman really wants to help you, her cottage doesn't seem very safe. The soldiers are sure to search it. The girl who warned you probably knows a safe place to hide. You decide to follow her.

You shake your head at the woman in the doorway and run as fast as you can across the town square. As you rush down a path between two fields, you can hear the soldiers shouting. They've spotted you!

You race down the narrow path. The sound of running men and hoofbeats tells you that the soldiers are close behind. You don't dare look back for fear of tripping on the uneven ground.

Up ahead is a thick grove of trees. If you can just reach it, maybe you can find someplace to hide.

As you get near the trees, you stumble on a rock and fall flat. You lie there, stunned, waiting for the soldiers to catch up and haul you off to the Tower.

"Don't lie there like a fool!" whispers a high-pitched voice.

With a shock, you feel a strong hand haul you to your feet.

See who it is on PAGE 35.

The tunnel slopes down gently. It's easy to walk. But soon it's pitch-black, and you start to wonder if you should turn back.

Then you see a shape ahead. In the dim light it looks like a person, but as you get closer you realize it's only part of one — a skeleton. The bones are charred and blackened. The smell of burned flesh fills your nostrils.

"This person's been burned!" you cry out loud.

"That's right!"

You jump in fright, your heart pounding with fear.

The skeleton is talking to you!

Turn to PAGE 86.

You haven't followed this road for more than ten minutes before you come to a large wooden sign. The crudely drawn letters are hard to read, but you can make them out.

DRAGON'S CAVE
TURN BACK OR PERISH.

You want to laugh out loud. These medieval people are so stupid! They actually believe in dragons.

Then you notice that the edges of the sign are charred black. You peer past the sign and you see that the trees behind it are burned like matchsticks.

Eddie and Sue didn't say anything about a dragon's cave, you think. But it's on their map.

If I were going to hide something, I'd put it here.

Then again, those burned trees . . . and the charred sign . . .

What if there really is such a thing as a dragon?

If you go to the cave, turn to PAGE 51.

If you turn back, or if you already have two stones, go to PAGE 69.

"We'll just have to figure out what magic powers the old king has, won't we?" you say, trying to sound confident.

Eddie and Sue nod in agreement. Carefully, the three of you slip out of the room. You start down the stairs. But instead of going all the way to the bottom, Eddie opens a secret door halfway down.

"Our father showed us this before he died," Eddie explains. "It leads to the castle."

The thought of going to the castle makes your heart sink. But how else are you going to defeat King Robert?

"Ready?" Eddie says, just before he ducks into the doorway.

"Right behind you," Sue tells him.

"Right behind you," you echo nervously.

Go to PAGE 22.

Wait! you think just as you're about to say the letters out loud. That message is in *code*! And the + 2 is the key to the code.

Quickly you translate the letters, changing each one for the letter that comes two after it in the alphabet.

Write the answer here:

_m o r g R E d_

Kmpepcb +2

@ be

morgred

Now turn to PAGE 45.

32

You are standing in the middle of a crossroads. Tall trees surround you. From where you stand, six roads branch off in six different directions.

Alongside each road is a stone marker with a simple picture carved in it. You study the markers for a long while. What do the signs mean? Which road leads to the stones? Which leads to the Tower?

You study your map. Then you glance back at the stone markers. Which one will lead to success — and which will lead to death?

Which road do you take?

If you take the road marked *, go to PAGE 61.*

If you take the road marked *, go to PAGE 60.*

If you take the road marked *, go to PAGE 84.*

If you take the road marked *, go to PAGE 29.*

If you take the road marked *, go to PAGE 44.*

If you take the road marked *, go to PAGE 130.*

"Okay. Let's eat!" you decide.

The stranger leads you to a table and motions for you to sit. Then the stranger throws back the hood of the cloak.

To your astonishment, the stranger is not a man at all. It's a young woman with long red hair.

"I am Robin," she announces with a broad grin. "And these are my people, all sworn enemies of King Robert and the Lord High Executioner."

Dozens of men and women crowd around. You notice that the looks they give you are not all friendly.

"Now that you know who I am," Robin continues, "it's time to tell us who you are, stranger."

You know you have to be careful, but you want to trust these people. You need a friend in this strange place and time. So the words begin to pour out of you.

You tell the whole story — about Eddie and Sue and the time travel and how you are trying to rescue them. When you're done, the crowd of people stares at you, dumbfounded.

"A strange story," Robin says thoughtfully. "And we would like to help the prince and princess if we can. But how do we know we can believe you?"

Go to PAGE 83.

Proudly, you pull the two remaining stones from your book bag and hold them out. "Here they are!" you shout.

Eddie hands you his. Now you have all three.

"You did it!" Sue cries. "I knew you could!"

BAM! The stone door shakes and cracks.

"It's the Executioner!" Sue cries. "Run!"

She dashes to a door in the opposite wall. You all rush through and run down a long tunnel, then up a flight of creaking wooden stairs.

The door gives its last groan. You hear the Executioner and his men shouting as they rush down the long tunnel after you.

"Go!" Eddie shrieks. "Run faster!"

Gasping, you reach the last stair. And stumble!

The precious magic stones fly out of your hand and bounce across the floor. You grasp at them desperately.

By the time you have all the stones, Eddie and Sue are gone.

Now the soldiers are running up the steps!

Think! You have the stones. You could use them to escape.

Or you could try to catch up with Eddie and Sue. Can you outrun those furious soldiers?

If you use the stones, turn to PAGE 115.

If you try to catch up with Eddie and Sue, race to PAGE 82.

You peer up at a slender figure in a dark cloak and hood.

"Come on, then!" he whispers. "Or do ye want to be taken to the Tower?"

You only have a split second to make your decision. But it's not much of a choice. You allow yourself to be pulled into the shelter of a stand of thin birch trees. The man roughly shoves you to the ground. Then he drops down next to you. In the next second, a troop of armored horsemen thunder by on the narrow lane. They're followed by a dozen foot soldiers. You can hear the men grunt as they run down the path.

You can hardly breathe from fear. The man next to you claps a hand on your shoulder.

"Come on, then," he says as he gets to his feet. Without another word, he begins to walk deeper into the forest. If he's following a trail, you don't see it. You get up and stumble after the stranger. His face is hidden by his hood, but you notice that he's not much taller than you are.

"Where are we going?" you gasp as you struggle to keep up.

"Robin's Camp," is his only reply.

Follow him to PAGE 78.

You reach into your book bag and pull out your reflective sunglasses.

"These will protect me," you say, slipping on the sunglasses. You're trying to act confident. But your heart is beating a mile a minute. "I'll try to distract him. You guys go for the stone. Then we'll run for it."

You're so scared, you don't want to give yourself time to change your mind. You jump from your hiding place.

"Hey, Executioner," you sneer. "It doesn't look like you're getting anywhere very fast."

The evil nobleman doesn't look surprised to see you. He smiles cruelly, and his steely gray eyes bore into you.

"I've been looking for you," he says in a smooth, clear voice. "Come to me."

You feel as though an unseen hand is drawing you closer to him. Your legs and arms grow heavy. You have trouble thinking.

Go to PAGE 10.

THUD!

You fall to the ground with an impact that knocks the breath out of you. The wooden floor beneath you is now cold, rough stone. It's dark except for a flicker of firelight from nearby.

"UGGA POBRA!"

A harsh voice makes you jump to your feet. You're face-to-face with a short, very muscular man. All he's wearing is a dirty animal skin around his waist. His hair and beard hang around his shoulders in long, greasy knots. He waves a stone ax at you and bares his teeth in a growl.

Nervously you glance around. You're in a cave. There's a large fire in the middle of the floor, and behind the man are a dozen other people — men, women, and children — all in animal skins.

I'm back in the Stone Age! you realize with dismay. *That spell. The book said it's where everybody starts! It meant all people started in the Stone Age. That's not fair!*

"UGGA POBRA!" the caveman roars, lifting his ax.

If an anthropologist finds your bones hundreds of thousands of years from now, it will change the study of ancient man.

And my teacher said I'd never amount to anything, you think, just as the stone ax swings toward your head.

THE END

38

You crash into the warm, swampy water of the moat. The shouts of the guards are muffled as you sink beneath the surface.

A second later, your feet touch the slimy bottom. You push off and stroke away from the drawbridge.

You fight to stay underwater as long as you can. Finally, your lungs are bursting. You have to come up for air.

You slip to the surface. You've only managed to get a few yards from the drawbridge. The soldiers and the nobleman are lined up along the bridge. But instead of trying to capture you, they're just watching silently. You twist around in the water, struggling to get a glimpse of what they're searching for.

"The creature will eat well today!" one of the soldiers shouts into the silence. The guards all laugh coldly.

The creature? you repeat to yourself. Uh-oh.

Sink to PAGE 119.

"Who are you?" you ask, still feeling groggy.

"I'm Mr. Congreve," he says in an icy tone. "Assistant manager. And I was about to ask you what you're doing sleeping in one of our rooms."

"Your rooms?" you repeat dumbly. You gaze around.

Everything has changed! You're not in Morgred's Tower anymore. You're in some sort of hotel room. There's a television, and a phone by the bed, and the assistant manager is wearing modern clothes. You're back in your own time! But how?

The manager frowns. "This is the Barclay Hotel, London." He sniffs. "And our rooms are only for our paying guests."

Your mind races as you try to figure out what happened. You were sitting on Morgred's bed and you said, "I could sleep for about eight hundred years." The next thing you knew . . .

Of course! Morgred had a magic bed. It put you to sleep for as long as you wanted.

You've been asleep for eight hundred years!

"Come along," the manager says. "You'll have to leave."

As you stand up to follow the manager you realize that you'll never rescue Edward and Susannah now.

Eight hundred years, you think as you leave the room. I just hope they don't make me pay the hotel bill!

THE END

40

You step toward the door. But then you catch a glimpse of your jeans and sneakers.

I can't go outside like this! you think. Your heart is beating quickly. Eddie and Sue told the truth about time travel. That means their story about King Robert and his scary sidekick — the Lord High Executioner — is also true. You're in real danger! Any mistake could mean death or . . . a living death in the Tower.

You peer around the room. Your book bag is on the small wooden table. Next to it is a piece of loose-leaf paper.

You grab the paper and carry it to the low doorway, where there's more light. It's a note from Eddie and Sue.

> *We have gone to the village for supplies. If we are not back by the time you wake up, then we probably have been captured by the Lord High Executioner. He will take us to the Tower. But he will not kill us until he has all the stones. We have kept one and hidden two — we can't write where, in case this note falls into the wrong hands. They are in two of the places on the map.*
>
> *Our fate rests in your hands. Only you can help. You must find the stones and then rescue us from the Tower.*

"The Tower?" you gasp.

Read more on PAGE 91.

You snap the book's cover shut.

"I am not messing around with this stuff," you say out loud.

"Good choice!"

You whirl around. With a shock you realize the skeleton in the corner is talking. Its jaw clatters up and down.

"You are not ready for the book," it goes on. "But I'm going to reward you for knowing your own limits."

The skeleton points a white finger bone at a wooden box in the corner. You walk over and study the box. There's an egg-shaped dent in the lid.

"If you have a magic white stone, you may place it in the dent," the skeleton chatters. "And then you'll get a big surprise!"

A big surprise? Hmmmm. Sometimes surprises aren't all they're cracked up to be. Especially in the Middle Ages!

If you have a magic stone and you want to put it in the hole in the lid, turn to PAGE 94.

If you don't have a magic stone, or if you do have it but you don't want to use it, turn to PAGE 69.

Cautiously, you follow the road. Soon you come to a small rise. Below you is a village. It's just a collection of huts with thatched roofs and mud walls. Thin gray smoke rises from the chimneys. Chickens peck in the dirt.

This is where the common people live, you think as you walk toward the huts. I wonder if Sue and Eddie came here? They might have left one of the stones with someone they trust.

The road leads into a square of packed brown dirt at the center of the village.

Just as you reach it, you hear shouting and scuffling. Soldiers? You brace yourself. Then a pack of seven or eight kids comes racing around the corner of one of the cottages. Some are really young, but the oldest one looks like a teenager. They're all wearing tattered clothes covered with soot and grime.

"Who's that?" screeches one of the little kids.

The whole gang stops. Quickly, they fan out and form a ring around you. Before you know it, you're surrounded. They stare at you silently.

You stare back. What should you do? What should you say? How will these kids from the Middle Ages react to a stranger?

Turn to PAGE 89.

You take a deep breath and join the mass of people on the main road toward the castle. You push your way through the crowded market square. The air is thick with the smells of cooking food, animal skins, and unwashed people.

Soon you're standing just below the drawbridge. A short line has formed as people wait to get past the guards. Just ahead, two fierce-looking soldiers grab a farmer by his arms and yank a large basket from his grip.

"What have you got there?" one of the guards sneers.

"J-j-just chickens," the peasant stammers. "For the royal kitchen."

With a harsh laugh, one of the guards turns the basket over, dumping the squawking hens onto the planks of the drawbridge.

"His Majesty don't want scrawny-looking things like this," the guard says. He kicks the hens into the water of the moat.

"But —" the farmer protests.

"Are you making trouble?" the guard shouts. "You know where we take troublemakers, don't you?" He points toward the Tower.

Without a word, the farmer turns and slinks away, stumbling past you into the crowd.

"Who's next?" roars the guard, laughing with delight. He glares at you.

Go to PAGE 121.

44

This road leads toward a tower. As you walk along, it quickly turns into nothing more than a narrow trail through jumbled underbrush. The thorny bushes crowd in around you. Before you've walked very far, your arms and face are scratched and bleeding in a dozen places.

You're tired and hot, and the cuts sting. Just as you decide to go back to the crossroads to find an easier route, you see a tall, slender tower on a hill high above you.

"The Terror Tower!" you moan out loud.

But it doesn't look the way you imagined. It's white and pretty and almost inviting. There are even pink and white flowers growing around the base.

You decide to take a closer look. After a few minutes of climbing, you reach the base of the Tower. There are no windows, and there's only one small wooden door.

You circle the Tower. The door is the only way in.

You walk toward the door. It's made of rough, unfinished wood, without a handle or even a knocker. It's set deep in the stone wall. You notice the stones around the entrance are jagged, almost like teeth.

Go to PAGE 134.

Now you know what the coded message means. In a loud, clear voice, you shout, "MORGRED!"

The door swings open by itself, and you see a clean, well-lit, round room inside.

"Of course," you declare. "This isn't Terror Tower. It's Morgred's Tower. Morgred is the wizard who helped Edward and Susannah. The guy who pretends to be their father, Mr. Morgan."

Morgred is back in your own time. But he's a friend of the prince and princess. Maybe there's something in his tower you can use to help rescue them.

Feeling relieved, you step over the threshold.

The room you enter seems to be Morgred's living area. There's a simple bed, a table and two chairs, a fireplace, and some pots and pans. There's also a wooden staircase leading to the next floor.

If you go up the stairs, go to PAGE 74.

If you decide to explore this room more, go to PAGE 66.

"Let's get the stone first," you say. "At least then we'll have a way of escaping the Lord High Executioner. Later we can see about overthrowing the king."

Eddie and Sue nod in agreement. A moment later the three of you are slipping down the stone staircase. About halfway down, Eddie pulls your arm. He and Sue lead you into a secret doorway that you missed on your way up.

"These steps lead to the dungeon," he whispers. "The Executioner has probably hidden our stone down there."

You keep walking until it seems that you must be deep beneath the earth. Suddenly Eddie shoves his arm in front of you. With a shock, you see why he's stopped. On the curved wall of the staircase is a shadow — the outline of a tall, thin, cloaked figure. The light is coming from a large chamber just below you.

Without being told, you know who the shadow belongs to: the Lord High Executioner.

Tiptoe to PAGE 55.

"All right," you agree slowly. "What do I have to do?"

The tall servant hands you a large wooden bucket filled with black lumps of coal. It's so heavy, it almost pulls your arm from its socket. The leather handle bites into your palm.

"Take this to the southwest guardroom. Use the stairs by the north wall. Count off fifteen paces at the third landing. Go through the second archway to the northeast. Go down the first ladder and over the buttress to the second battlement. Watch your step on the rain gutter. Drop off the coal. And hurry back!"

You're about to ask him to repeat the directions when he raises his meaty fist above your head.

"Step lively before I box your ears!" he bellows.

You can tell he means it, so you stagger off with your load. It takes all your effort to haul the bucket up the stairs. Soon you lose count of the landings.

You're lost.

You remember that the skinny servant said something about going down a ladder, so when you see one, you climb down. You find yourself in a long tunnel, lined with damp stone walls.

"I think I'm supposed to go this way," you mutter to yourself as you tramp down the dark, cold tunnel.

Turn to PAGE 87.

You find yourself in a large underground chamber. It's pretty dark, but some light comes down through a hole in one of the walls. You realize you must be near the surface.

The cavern is empty except for something small and white that sits in the middle of the floor. You rush to it and pick it up. It's a small white stone, about the size of an egg. It starts to glow in your palm.

"It's one of the magic stones!" you cry. "Yes!" Joy floods through you. Carefully, you slip it into your pocket. Then you look around for a way out.

The light is coming from a sloping shaft that leads up. Its sides are smooth and slippery. You try to inch up. Right away you slip and fall to the ground. Jagged rocks bruise your back.

Maybe I could climb that if I tried a little harder, you think.

Or maybe next time I'll fall and break my legs.

There are several other holes in the wall, but all of them lead downward. You see one tunnel that looks large enough to stand in. The path seems much easier. Which way do you go?

If you go up the shaft, turn to PAGE 23.
If you go down the tunnel, go to PAGE 28.

You plunge your hand into your book bag, fish around, and pull out your flashlight.

"B-b-behold!" you say, trying to sound as if you're about to show the dragon something great. "A magic light stick!"

The dragon turns its head so one of its huge green eyes is turned toward the flashlight.

"A light stick?" it breathes, and a ball of orange fire explodes out of its mouth with a tremendous *CRACK*. "How does the magic work?"

"Like this, oh fire breather!" you reply. You switch on the flashlight. The beam of light shoots right into the dragon's eye.

With a gigantic roar of pain, the dragon snaps its head backwards. The force of its breath knocks you tumbling to the floor. You feel the soles of your boots curl up from the heat.

"A trick!" the dragon roars. "You have tried to blind me! Now you will feel my flames!"

The giant head comes at you like a freight train. The huge mouth opens. You can smell the sickening stench of the dragon's fiery breath. You turn to run, but as you do, the dragon opens its mouth. When you hear the roar of its breath, you turn — just in time to see a gigantic ball of fire flying through the air. And it's headed straight for you!

THE END

You'll never get a chance like this again. You have to get that key! You yank down the heavy velvet curtain and fling it at Lord Worcester. Startled, he steps back, then crashes to the ground, tangled in the material.

You don't have a second to lose. You dash into the next room, grab the key, and run to another door. You leap through and clamber up the steep stone steps on the other side. Behind you, Worcester calls for help.

You reach the top of the stairs and run through another doorway. You're on a small balcony looking out over . . . the Throne Room! King Robert, the noblemen and ladies of the court, and dozens of guards stare up at you. Then they all start shouting.

You glance around wildly. You spot a thick rope hanging from a bracket on the wall next to you. It's used to raise and lower the chandelier in the center of the hall. Maybe you can use the rope to swing to the balcony on the other side of the room.

You peek down at the Throne Room, a good fifty feet below you. If you fall, you're a goner. But in another minute, you'll be captured. You grab the rope and leap out into space.

The Throne Room rushes by in a blur as you swing through the air. The balcony on the opposite wall comes closer . . . closer. . . .

Leap to PAGE 96.

You take a deep breath and walk past the sign and into the burned forest. The land becomes more and more barren, until there's nothing but rocks, burned soil, and pools of muddy water.

The path leads down into a grim-looking valley. At the bottom, in a cleft between two large boulders, is a gaping hole.

That must be it, you think, although you've never seen a dragon's cave before.

You clamber over the stones and drop into the black mouth of the cave.

You thought it would be dark as night inside, but instead it is brightly lit. You gasp when you see that the light is coming from a mountain of jewels and gold piled on the floor of the cavern. Then a rush of hot air and a sound like a blast furnace shock you back to reality.

Above the jewels rises a long, snakelike neck, and at the end of the neck is a lizardlike head — only this head is the size of a small car. Bright orange and blue flames leap from its mouth and nose as it speaks.

"Who dares disturb me?" it thunders.

Whoa! Guess there is such a thing as a dragon, after all.

Kick yourself on PAGE 25.

52

This isn't a movie, you remind yourself. Just because they're wearing green tights doesn't mean they're like Robin Hood.

You slowly back away from the smiling men.

"Uh, I just remembered," you say. "I'm not very hungry."

"Oh, come now," the leader of the men says, taking a quick step toward you. "Just a quick bite."

"Uh, no, thanks," you repeat. You sense someone behind you and turn. It's the one called Little John. He smiles down at you, and suddenly you notice that he has very sharp teeth.

Without stopping to think, you kick the big man in the knee.

"Yeow!" he howls. You dodge around him.

You run down the road as fast as you can, your heart beating wildly. There's something wrong with these guys.

You glance over your shoulder. They're gaining on you. You know you can't outrun them.

"Okay, you big bullies!" you shout, whirling around. You're ready to fight, even though it seems hopeless. But to your surprise, the men run right by you.

"Guess they're not as tough as I thought," you say.

"No, they're not," someone answers.

Turn to PAGE 19.

"I'm *so* out of here," you tell Eddie and Sue. You stand up and walk toward the kitchen door.

"Wait!" Sue cries. "We need your help!"

"My help?" you answer. "I think you both need help from someone else — like maybe a shrink!"

You push through the screen door and pick up your bike, which was lying on the Morgans' front lawn.

As you pedal down the road, you breathe a big sigh of relief. Wow, you think, my friends are really losing it!

Unfortunately, they're also your only friends in the neighborhood. After you pedal around alone for an hour, you decide to head home.

What a bore, you think, flopping onto the couch in your den. Hanging out alone really stinks.

And in this *GIVE YOURSELF GOOSE-BUMPS* book, it also means

THE END.

You have no idea what's behind that curtain. And being Lord Worcester's page has worked out pretty well so far. You slip behind the earl's cape and sit down.

Your eyes are filled with the sparkle of gold jewelry, the rich colors of thick tapestries hanging from the walls, the glinting armor of the palace guards.

You feel relaxed as you wait to see what will happen next. At that moment, the earl takes a step forward, toward the throne.

"Sire!" he calls.

From his seat on the throne, King Robert glances up quickly.

"Yes, Lord Worcester?" he asks.

"Sire, when you asked about your niece and nephew I forgot to mention something." The earl smiles pleasantly.

"Please," King Robert says with an impatient wave of his hand. "Worcester, do you always have to be so dramatic?"

"My apologies, Sire," Worcester answers with a deep bow. "It's just that I don't often get to unmask a traitor!"

Traitor? You wonder who the earl can be talking about.

Then you notice he is pointing at you!

Go to PAGE 56.

Silently, hugging the wall, the three of you creep downward. Soon you can see a large room at the foot of the stairs. The Executioner is standing next to a large table. In front of him is a round white stone. He stands over it, moving his long, thin hands back and forth, mumbling words.

"He's trying to travel in time with only one stone," Sue whispers to you. "It will never work."

"He's alone," Eddie whispers. "This is our chance to steal the stone."

"No! He's too powerful," Sue protests. "If you gaze into his eyes, you'll be hypnotized. You know that."

"It's true," Eddie says. "All his power is in his eyes. They're very sensitive. That's why he stays in dark places. If only there was some way to avoid his gaze."

The stone glows in the dim light of the chamber. In spite of your fear, you want to reach out and grab it. If only there was a way to avoid the Executioner's hypnotic sight!

Is there something in your book bag you can use?

If you have the sunglasses, turn to PAGE 36.
If you don't have them, go to PAGE 26.

Before you can move, four heavily armed royal guards appear at your side.

"This is one of your niece and nephew's friends," the earl tells the king with a flourish.

King Robert gets to his feet and glares at you.

"A friend of theirs, are you?" he shouts. "You'll wish you had better friends when we're done with you."

"This spy was disguised as a peasant," Worcester continues. "But I have ways of seeing those who have used the magic stones. This one stood out as clear as day."

"Good work," the king says with a smile. "But, then, I expect such work from the Lord High Executioner."

An icy finger of fear travels down your spine. Worcester is the Lord High Executioner — the same man Eddie and Sue warned you about. The one who imprisoned them in the Tower. And you walked right into his clutches!

You're on the way to the Tower yourself. Your heart sinks with the knowledge of what awaits you.

"You should have stayed in your own time," the Lord High Executioner sneers. "We may seem primitive to you in this age, but there's one thing we're much better at — causing pain!"

THE END

Oh, no! The woman betrayed you!

The lid of the basket is thrown back, and you stare up into the faces of five armored soldiers. They all laugh wickedly.

You feel icy terror spread through you. You've been captured by the king's men. It won't take long for them to figure out you're not from this time. Then they'll hand you over to the Lord High Executioner. And that means — the Tower.

"Hey!" the woman yells angrily as they drag you outside. "What about me reward?"

The commander flips her a dull copper-colored coin. She snaps it out of the air and squints at it.

"I got three times this for the last one," she says.

"The price has gone down," the soldier laughs harshly.

"The *last* one?" you blurt out.

The soldier chuckles. "Princess Susannah."

You gasp. This woman betrayed Sue.

And you fell into the same trap!

With all these guards there's no chance of escaping. As they tie you to the back of a horse, you can't help your next thought.

The woman got three times as much for betraying Sue.

So what am I? Chopped liver?

THE END

"Come along!" the man calls. He twirls his staff like a baton. "Knock me in, or I'll knock you in!"

A dozen hands push you onto the tree trunk. It isn't more than two feet wide. It's all you can do to keep your balance. How are you going to fight this giant man?

He takes a step forward and swings the end of his staff at your head. You manage to duck as it goes whistling by above you. The crowd cheers.

"Hey!" you think. "Maybe I have a chance to —"

Your thoughts are cut off by a nasty crack as the other end of the man's staff hits you on the ankle. Your feet go flying out into space. You grab for the tree trunk. But it's no use. The last thing you hear before you hit the water is wild cheering.

The rushing water drags you along. You fight to keep your head above the surface. Finally the current throws you up against the bank, and you crawl ashore.

You lie there panting and spitting out the water you've swallowed. Finally, after a long while, you recover. You haul yourself up the riverbank and find yourself by a small footpath. You follow it. Before long you are right back where you started — at the crossroads.

Turn to PAGE 32.

As soon as you step through the entrance, you're hit by a wall of noise and commotion. Pots are banging, geese and ducks are squawking, and everywhere people are shouting over the din. A blast of hot air strikes you in the face. The heavy smell of burned flesh fills your nostrils.

For a moment you think you've stumbled into some terrible dungeon. Then some of the smoke swirling around you clears, and you realize you're just in the castle's main kitchen. Servants are rushing everywhere, some with live animals, some with trays heaped with food. The stink is overpowering. As you stand there blinking, a tall, skinny man in a grease-stained apron rushes up to you.

"There you are!" he shouts over the noise. "I told them we wanted new help, but you aren't much to look at. Still, I suppose you'll do. Don't stand there gawking. There's work to be done!"

You can only stare at him openmouthed. Somehow he thinks you're a new servant sent to work in the kitchen.

Hey, this could be your chance to get farther into the castle! But on the other hand, you could wind up spending the rest of the day washing dishes.

If you agree to work, turn to PAGE 47.

If you tell Skinny you don't want the job, turn to PAGE 11.

You know where this road leads. To a tower — and you fear it must be Terror Tower.

This cobblestone road is wide and smooth. It runs arrow-straight. After a few minutes, you come out of a valley and see where the road is taking you. King Robert's huge castle stands in the distance. But the road doesn't go to the castle's main gate.

Instead it leads to a tall, windowless black tower.

"Terror Tower," you mutter. "The Tower of the Lord High Executioner."

Gathering your nerve, you walk on. You see two guards standing by the side of the road. You take a deep breath and keep walking. Then you see that they're not real guards, just statues.

Weird.

Finally you come to the Tower's tall, ironbound doorway. Several of the stone guards stand on either side, but there is no sign of anything living. In the door is a keyhole and a knob.

Part of you wants to turn and run, but you know that sooner or later, this is where your search will lead you.

Are you ready to enter?

If you want to pick another path, turn to PAGE 69.

If you have a key, go to PAGE 75.

If you turn the doorknob, go to PAGE 123.

I'll head this way, you decide.

You strike off down a broad, well-tended road. Eventually it becomes paved with smooth gray cobblestones, and the walking is easier. The sun is shining.

Soon the road starts getting crowded. Rich lords and ladies, dressed in silks and velvets, are riding on big horses. Peasants dressed in heavy woolen clothes balance large loads on their shoulders. Beggars dressed in rags stumble along, asking for handouts.

They're all heading in the same direction. The road becomes even more crowded. As you climb to the top of a hill, you understand why.

In the green valley below is a huge stone castle. It looks like something out of a fairy tale.

Then you see that at one corner of the castle stands a black, windowless tower. You shiver. You know from Eddie and Sue's description that it's Terror Tower. Your steps are bringing you closer to the last place you want to be!

But you have to face it eventually. You follow the crowd down the road toward the castle.

Go on to PAGE 85.

You don't have time to play games with these kids.

"Sorry," you answer. "But I can't play now. I, uh, I have homework to do."

He stares at you. "Homework?" he asks. "What is that?"

The big boy turns and wanders off. Most of the kids follow him. But two stay — a boy and a girl who both look about your age.

"Homework?" the boy says, squinting at you. He scratches his head with a filthy hand. "I knows a place you can do homework. Come along with me. It's not far."

He grins. His teeth are yellow, and there are a couple missing. But his smile seems friendly.

"Don't go with him," the girl says. "His place is on the other side of the village. If the king's soldiers spot you, they will stop you. And question you. And if they don't like the answers . . ." She makes a cutting motion across her throat with her index finger.

She's right. The last thing you want is to run into some of the king's men. Maybe you should find a place to hide out.

But that won't help you find Eddie and Sue. Maybe you should follow the boy. You could ask him some questions.

If you go with the boy, turn to PAGE 125.
If you decide to hide, turn to PAGE 7.

"Here, oh mighty breath!" you say in a quivering voice. "A magic music machine!"

Your hands are shaking, but you manage to pull your tape player from your book bag.

"Music?" the dragon replies. Maybe it's wishful thinking, but the creature sounds a little less angry.

"Make music!" it commands you.

"Uh, you have to wear it," you explain nervously.

You creep up the pile of jewels until you are level with one of the beast's ears. You feel the great neck twitching beneath you. As carefully as you can, you place the earphones on the leathery ear and tuck the tape player inside the ear itself. Then you switch on the tape and hold your breath.

Turn to PAGE 117.

You manage to sit up.

"Eddie? Sue?" you call. "Where are you? Are you all right?"

There's no reply at first. Then you hear a soft grunting noise, almost as if someone is trying to talk.

"Eddie?" you manage to call. "Is that you? Sue? Are you hurt?"

No answer. All you hear is the same muffled sound.

The sound is coming from outside. You stagger to your feet, still weak from the time travel.

Then you stop. You don't know what that noise is. You don't even know where you are. Who knows what's waiting outside the hut?

What do you do?

If you go outside, turn to PAGE 97.
If you stay where you are, turn to PAGE 40.

Your heart beating wildly, you turn and race across the nearest field. But the hulking soldiers quickly catch up. A fierce blow from behind sends you sprawling in the dirt.

Two of the men grab you roughly and haul you to your feet.

You struggle, but they hold you tight.

"Let me go!" you cry. "I didn't do anything wrong."

"Sure you did," the commander says with a wicked smile. "You're wearing them strange clothes. The same kind His Lordship told us to look for."

You glance down at your jeans and sneakers. With a sinking heart, you realize that your clothes gave you away. Eddie told you the Lord High Executioner had been to modern times. He knows which clothes to tell his men to look for.

"Don't worry about your clothes," the soldier sneers. "His Lordship will give you something else to wear once you're in the Tower. Like maybe a shirt full of spikes and nails!"

All the soldiers guffaw.

As they drag you away, you know you've failed even before you've begun. And soon you will know what it means to be a prisoner in Terror Tower.

THE END

I'd better go slowly, you think. I'll check out this room before I see what's upstairs.

It sounds like a good idea, but after a minute you start to get bored. All you find are some old pots and pans, knives and forks, and other kitchen utensils. There's a covered pot by the fireplace, but when you open it, your nose is hit by a terrible smell. Inside is a black-and-green gooey mess. You drop the pot and jump back in fright, expecting some more magic. Then you realize it's just some moldy food that Morgred left behind.

You're still recovering from your shock when you sit down on the wooden bed. It's covered with a soft woolen blanket. You bounce up and down a couple of times. Suddenly you realize how tired you are.

"I could sleep for about eight hundred years," you say out loud, with a yawn.

Before you know it, your eyes are drooping shut. Your arms and legs feel as if they're sinking into the bed. Your head drops to the pillow. . . .

"Wake up!"

Someone is shaking you. You open your eyes.

A man is standing over you. He's wearing a dark blue blazer, tan pants, a white shirt, and a striped tie.

Get out of bed on PAGE 39.

"I am taking you to the forest, Your Highness," Robin answers. "It's the only place you will be safe."

"Good idea!" Sue cries. "We will join your band. The forest will be our home until we can find a way to regain our rightful throne."

The forest? you think. With Robin Hood?

It sounds exciting, even though it means staying in the Middle Ages. After all, the third magic stone still exists. Maybe someday you'll be able to find it and get back to your own time and your own home.

Until then, you'll just have to make the best of it.

"We'll steal from the rich and give to the poor!" you shout, feeling excited.

"Hey," Robin says. "That's a great slogan! Mind if I use it?"

THE END

The main point of getting into the castle was to try to find Eddie and Sue. You can't do that here. While Worcester's attention is still on the king, you slip behind the purple curtain and through the narrow wooden door it conceals.

You find yourself in a small chamber lit by one sputtering candle. At the other end is another door, covered by another velvet curtain. You hear muffled voices.

You creep to the curtain and peek through. You see a slightly larger room. And two men standing in it.

"You won't do it?" demands one of them, a tall, thin man wearing a dark cloak that almost hides his face. "No one disobeys me! Am I not the Lord High Executioner?"

The Lord High Executioner!

The words echo in your brain. You're standing just a few feet away from the most feared and hated man in the kingdom.

The other man seems to be a nobleman, but he acts as scared of the Executioner as you feel.

"Your Lordship," he whines. "Ask me something else, I beg!"

"It must be done!" the Executioner hisses. He throws a large brass key onto the table. "This is the key to the Tower. Return it to me when you are done."

Hear more on PAGE 109.

You decide it might be a good idea to go back to the crossroads and choose another destination.

You start walking. An hour later, you find yourself back at the intersection of all the roads.

Turn to PAGE 32.

70   You take the portable tape player out of your pocket.

"This is from the future!" you proclaim. Confidently, you step to the nearest person, a young woman. You slip the headphones over her ears and switch on the tape.

"You see," you start to explain, "it plays —"

"Help!" The woman screams and snatches the headphones from her ears. "I heard demons. The box is black magic!"

"No," you assure her. "It's all very scientific. See, there's magnetic tape, which . . ."

But your words are drowned out by the screams of the people.

"Witchcraft!" they shout. "Burn the witch!"

"I'm not a witch," you wail, turning to Robin.

She glares at you with shock and anger. "Take the witch away," she commands.

A dozen pairs of hands grab you and lift you off the ground. You're tied to the stake with thick ropes. Others pile brush and firewood around your feet. There's nothing you can do, no way to escape. Then one of the men comes up, carrying a torch. He's going to set the woodpile on fire.

Then you remember what was in your cassette player — a homemade tape of your neighbor's horrible band.

No wonder the woman thought she'd heard demons!

THE END

You lunge forward. The amber amulet is on a chain around the king's neck. His eyes are wild with fright.

Your fingertips are inches from the amulet. You give a last grab at the swinging pendant.

And you feel it in your palm! You yank the chain off and hold the amulet tight.

In the next second, two soldiers draw their swords and hold them inches from your chest.

"Kill them!" the king commands. He rubs his neck where the chain snapped. "Kill them now!"

The soldiers' faces are clouded with anger. The razor-sharp tips of their swords move closer. You close your eyes, ready for the end.

Face your doom on PAGE 12.

You dribble sideways across the clearing, as if you're going to drive around the men. As you hoped, they all shift to the side, leaving a small gap between the third and fourth man. Seeing your chance, you pivot and kick in one swift motion.

The ball shoots across the line like a missile and slips through the gap.

"Yesss!" you shout. Everyone starts cheering and applauding.

"I believe you now," Robin says warmly. "The prince and princess told me to look for you. They said I would know you by the way you could kick a ball. They left this for you."

She holds out her hand, palm up, and shows you a smooth, round white stone. It glows in the dim light of the clearing.

"One of Morgred's stones!" you cry, gratefully taking it.

"And here's something else." Robin shows you a small silver whistle. "We too have our magic," she explains. "Blow this whistle anywhere in the kingdom and we will hear it. If we can, we will come to your aid. But use it carefully — it only works once. Good luck on your journey."

Two of Robin's men lead the way into the forest.

An hour later, you are standing back at the crossroads.

Go to PAGE 136 and write: Magic Stone and Magic Whistle. Then go to PAGE 32.

I can trust her, you think. She's putting herself in danger by hiding me. Maybe she feels sorry for me.

You rush into the small cottage. The woman slams the door shut after you.

"Quick!" she whispers hoarsely. "Hide in the kindling basket!"

She shoves you toward the back of the room, where a large wicker basket stands against the wall.

"Thank you so much —" you begin, but she motions you to be silent. She helps you climb into the basket. Then she drops the lid into place. You're in the dark. The twigs in the basket poke you in a dozen places, but you don't dare move.

Through the sides of the basket you hear the woman shuffling around in the cottage. Seconds later, you hear a heavy chain-mailed fist pounding on the thick cottage door.

"Open up in the name of the king!" booms a loud voice.

"All right! Ye don't have to shout!" the woman says. You hear her open the door.

I wonder what clever trick she's going to use to send them away, you think.

"I've got the one you're looking for," you hear the woman say matter-of-factly. "All wrapped up and ready to go."

Turn to PAGE 57.

You climb the steep stairs into another circular room. This one is full of glass beakers filled with colorful fluids. Herbs hang from the ceiling. A skeleton is propped in one corner.

In the center of the room is a large wooden table. It's bare except for a very thick, old book.

A spell book! you think, and run to the table. The words on the cover are in a strange script. But as you stare, the letters shift and change. Suddenly they stand out as clear as day.

> *WARNING! This book to be used only by trained magic technician. Unauthorized use may lead to unpredictable results. Above all, do not use the spell on page 2001! It is only for emergencies!*
>
> *Morgred.*

Unpredictable? you think. Everything that's happened lately is unpredictable. I need help.

But where do you start? The warning said the spell on page 2001 is for emergencies. Well, this is an emergency.

Then again, maybe you should start at the beginning of the book. Or should you heed the warning on the cover and not use the book at all?

If you want to start at the beginning of the book, turn to PAGE 9.

If you want to use the spell, go to PAGE 133.

If you don't want to use the book at all, go to PAGE 41.

You take out the brass key you found in the castle. With a shaking hand you slide it into the keyhole. You brace yourself for some kind of alarm to go off.

But the key fits in neatly. With a soft click you turn the lock, and the massive door swings open.

Inside, all you see is a dark corridor stretching before you. Taking a deep breath, you step over the threshold.

All by itself, the door swings shut behind you and locks with a loud *SNAP*.

You don't know whether you should be glad or scream in fright. But you made it.

You're inside Terror Tower.

Turn to PAGE 87.

"Me? Go to England eight hundred years in the past?" You laugh. "Why not? I was thinking of taking a bike ride, but a little time travel might be a nice change of pace."

Sue sighs.

"I know you don't believe us," she says, "but you will in a minute. I have proof." She digs into the pocket of her jeans. Then she lays three smooth white stones on the table. Each one is about the size of a chicken's egg.

"These are the stones that Morgred used to bring us to this time," she tells you.

You decide to play along. Maybe Sue and Eddie are about to pull some elaborate magic trick. That would be great!

"By the way," you pipe up, "where is Morgred? Is he coming on our little trip to the past?"

"No!" Eddie and Sue shout at once.

"He can't know our plan," Sue explains. "It's way too dangerous! He only told us what was happening to scare us into *never* going back."

"I see," you tell them. "Well? Use the stones! Let's go!"

Go to PAGE 129.

"Your home?" you reply, feeling dizzy. Has Worcester led you into a trap? You start to ask him, but Worcester waves his hand.

"There's no time for that," he commands. "Follow me. We must get away from here."

You don't have to be told twice. As you follow him down the dark tunnel, he begins to talk.

"I know you are a friend of the prince and princess. I too am their friend. Long ago, the king did me an injustice, and ever since I have been waiting to repay him. Now I'll get my revenge.

"You already have the key to the Tower. But I can tell you something that will help our friends. I know the secret of the king's power. It is a magic amulet, which contains an amber stone. If you can get the amulet away from him, his guards and the other nobles will no longer obey him. Instead, they will follow their true rulers — Edward and Susannah!"

It's all too strange — secret amulets, magic powers. You turn to Worcester in the darkness.

"You said the king did you an injustice," you demand. "Tell me, what was it? What did Robert do to you?"

Worcester gives you a strange look. Finally he speaks softly. "He had me killed."

Turn to PAGE 20.

Robin's camp? Could Robin be . . . Robin Hood?

You can't remember if there was a real Robin Hood. If there was, when did he live?

You walk through the dense woods for what seems like an hour. Then suddenly you emerge into a large clearing.

In front of you is a small village, tucked into the middle of the forest. Neat cottages are built around and sometimes in the trees. Tables are set out in the open, and dozens of people sit around them, eating, laughing, and talking.

"Robin's camp," your guide says with a flourish.

Right then you make up your mind. You're going to ask this fellow Robin to help you look for the stones.

"Please take me to see Robin," you ask.

"Now?" The stranger looks almost annoyed. "We haven't eaten."

"I have no time to waste," you reply, a little gruffly.

"Well, if you can't wait, go find Robin yourself," the stranger snaps.

You know you should find Robin. There's no time to waste. But you don't want to offend your guide, who's been helpful and kind. Besides, you're hungry!

If you go to find Robin, turn to PAGE 122.
If you stay with the stranger, go to PAGE 33.

"Yes, Sire!" shouts a guardsman. "To the Tower with them!"

"Wait!" the king commands. He points to you. "Bring that one to me."

The guard forces you to kneel before the king.

"You seem to enjoy leaping and dancing around my Throne Room," King Robert says. His face is red with anger. "Very well, dance for me now!"

"Dance?" you repeat, feeling confused.

"Guards!" the king commands. "Form a ring of steel."

At once, twenty guards draw their swords and surround you. You're standing in the middle of a circle of razor-sharp blades, all pointed at you.

"Dance!" the king commands. "And if you stop, you die!"

You hesitate, and immediately each soldier steps closer.

Feeling dazed and frightened, you begin to shuffle your feet. You tap and jump and whirl around. All the time, you're trying to think of a way out. But there is no way out.

"Dance, fool!" the king calls out. The crowd laughs.

You start to get tired. But when you slow down, the swords close in tighter. Soon the steel points are only inches from your ribs and back.

Ah, what the heck, you think. And you go out moon-walking.

THE END

You're blinded. A force like an invisible hand squeezes the air out of your lungs. You gasp for breath, fighting to stay awake. The room is spinning.

Fear and panic fill your mind. Whatever is happening is no game. But what is it? Magic?

Through the white haze that covers your vision, you can just make out Eddie in front of you. The three white stones are still in the palm of his hand, glowing fiercely.

The stones! you think. If I knock them down, whatever is happening will stop!

With all your might you struggle to lift your hand and knock away the stones. Then you remember what Sue said:

... whatever happens, don't touch the stones.

You hesitate. Sue told you not to touch them. But you feel as if you're choking to death! You've got to stop this!

What should you do?

If you knock down the stones, go to PAGE 116.
If you obey Sue's warning, go to PAGE 98.

You pull the soccer ball out of your book bag. The tall boy's eyes grow wide with wonder. "What be that?" he asks.

"A soccer ball," you answer. With a quick motion, you drop it and kick it toward him. The ball bounces off his chest and rolls away on the dirt.

"Oh!" the boy's face brightens. "A hitting game!"

You start to relax. You can make friends with these kids by teaching them soccer. You sort them into two teams.

Before long, all of you are racing up and down the dirt square. The kids catch on quickly. You're hot and dusty, but you're actually having fun.

You race toward the goal, easily dribbling the ball through the legs of an astonished medieval kid. You hear someone shout, "Shoot! Shoot!"

Hey, they catch on fast! I must be a really good coach, you think proudly. You shoot the ball into the makeshift goal. Score!

You look up, waiting to hear the other kids cheer.

That's when you realize the person shouting "shoot" isn't one of the kids. It's an armored knight sitting on a tall black charger. He's giving an order to another soldier. An order to shoot. To shoot *you* — with a crossbow!

Turn to PAGE 6.

I don't know how to use these things, you think, shoving the stones into your pocket. You leap to your feet and run down the hall just as the soldiers reach the top of the stairs.

"Over here!"

It's Sue. She and Eddie are waiting for you. They grab your arms, and together you jump into a trapdoor in the floor. For a sickening moment you fall through blackness. Then you hit water. The three of you are in an underground stream.

"Hold on!" Eddie cries.

You're carried along by a swift current. A minute later you burst into bright sunlight. You float along until the Tower fades in the distance. Finally the river slows. The three of you wade to a bank and pull yourselves out of the water.

"I know a place we can hide," Sue says. She leads the two of you into a nearby stand of birch trees.

She turns to you. "Better give Edward the stones for safekeeping."

You hand them to Eddie. They clink into his palm.

"Okay, let's get going," you say. "I don't want to get caught by those creeps."

"We *are* going," Sue says with a smile. "But you're not coming."

Go to *PAGE 21*.

How can you convince these people that you told the truth, that you really are from the future? You frown. There must be something in your book bag, something that will amaze them and make them believe your weird tale. But what did you bring with you?

If you have the soccer ball, go to PAGE 103.
If you have the tape player, turn to PAGE 70.
If you have both, choose PAGE 70 or PAGE 103.

84

This road leads into a thick forest. Massive oak trees line both sides, and tangled bushes and saplings crowd around their bases. Branches meet overhead, shutting out the sunlight.

The road looks well traveled, but after an hour of walking, you still haven't seen anyone. You are getting tired and thirsty.

SNAP!

Without warning, your feet are pulled out from under you. You're jerked up into the air, where you hang upside down.

You've walked into some sort of trap!

Desperately you twist around, trying to find a way to untie yourself. As you turn helplessly, a pair of dirty, sandal-clad feet come into view.

"Well, well, Little John!" says a man's voice. "It seems your trap caught something."

You raise your head and catch a glimpse of the speaker. He's tall and has a brown beard and shoulder-length hair. He's wearing a green tunic and leggings. On his head is a green hat with a long red feather.

"Welcome to our forest!" he says with a big grin.

Swing to PAGE 113.

As the road heads down into the valley and toward the castle, you see that it divides into two. The main branch heads through a bustling market, over the moat's drawbridge, and right through the main gates of the castle. Dozens of soldiers are guarding the entrance.

This must be King Robert's castle, you think.

You glance at the smaller road. It follows the castle wall for a while. Then it disappears around the corner. You don't know where it leads.

Which way should you go?

If you go to the main gate, turn to PAGE 43.

If you go to the smaller road, turn to PAGE 111.

If you want to return to the crossroads, go to PAGE 69.

The skeleton turns its eyeless skull toward you.

"This is what happens to those who are burned by a dragon," it declares. Its voice is harsh and brittle.

"A d-d-d-dragon?" you stammer.

"Of course. Don't you know you've stumbled into the dragon's cave?" the skeleton demands.

It shambles toward you. "I'll take your skin," it announces.

In horror, you turn to run. But your way is blocked by another blackened, charred skeleton, and then another. You're surrounded by them. They reach for you with their fire-blackened fingers. Their crumbling skin is falling on you in sheets.

"We need new skin!" one of them moans.

Oh, no! They're going to strip your body!

They grab hold of you. They pull at your flesh. You're being skinned alive!

"Help!" you shout. But there's no one to hear.

Well, you know what they say: Beauty is only skin-deep. It's what's inside that counts.

You just hope they're right!

THE END

You walk ahead in the darkness, feeling your way with your hand on the cold stone wall. You almost fall flat on your face when you come to a flight of steps leading up. You see a dim light coming from above. You stop and listen, straining to hear the sound of anyone who might be above you. But all you hear is your own breathing.

You start to climb slowly.

The light grows with each step you take. The stairs curve around, so you can't see what's ahead of you. And they start to narrow, until you feel the walls closing in. You have to fight back the panic that almost overwhelms you. This is Terror Tower!

As you come around one more curve, you see that your way is blocked by a door. This one is completely smooth. There's no keyhole, no doorknob, not even a crack or a seam.

You put the coal down and throw your shoulder against the door. But it's like pushing on solid rock. There's no way you can force it open. You have to turn around and go back down the stairs. Unless . . .

If you have the magic scroll, go to PAGE 107.
If you don't have it, go to PAGE 124.

You raise your flashlight, which you've hidden in your pocket, and shine it at the spot where you last saw the Executioner. The white beam of light cuts through the blackness.

For a brief second you're staring right into the Executioner's steely gray eyes.

But instead of hypnotizing you, his eyes close in pain.

"No!" he screams. "My eyes! You've blinded me!"

You turn away. At the same moment, you feel someone pulling on your sleeve.

"This way!" Sue urges. "Give me the flashlight!"

Using the beam, she leads you through a low doorway. Eddie is waiting on the other side. The three of you push the heavy stone door into place and bolt it shut.

You feel like shouting for joy. You can't believe you faced the Lord High Executioner and got away with it!

"I have it!" Eddie says, holding up the glowing white stone. He turns to you. "Where are the other two stones? Did you find them?"

If you have two of the magic stones, go to PAGE 34.

If you do not, go to PAGE 112.

You turn slowly, sizing up the gang of kids, trying to guess what they're going to do next. They look grim.

"Must be one of the king's spies," says a girl about your age. "Sent here to take more of our food."

They all mutter angrily. A few pick up rocks. The oldest boy takes a step toward you. He's at least a foot taller than you, and his arms bulge with muscles.

"Hey!" he barks. "What are you doing here? This be our place."

"I — I —" you stammer, trying to think of an answer. But your mind is a blank.

The boy takes another step forward. His face is covered with grime. His long brown hair is matted behind his ears. He also smells like he's been spending time with that pig back at the hut you woke up in.

The boy grins at you with yellow teeth. It's a nasty grin, not friendly. You get ready to run or fight if you have to.

And then the boy's grin gets wider.

"Know ye any good games?" he asks.

If you have the soccer ball, you can go to PAGE 81.

If you don't have the soccer ball — or if you have the ball but don't want to use it — go to PAGE 62.

CONK! The stone hits the wooden plank inches from your face. The crowd whoops and shouts.

"Let me out!" you plead.

"In a couple of days," sneers the tall servant from the kitchen. "If there's anything left of you."

A little kid steps up and throws a raw egg. It hits you right on the forehead. The crowd bursts into laughter.

Then a heavy clod of dirt strikes the board above your head. You feel the wet mud fall on your hair. Rocks and sticks fly at your face and body.

You're helpless. You can only close your eyes and brace yourself. You've forgotten about the stones and Eddie and Sue and getting home. All you care about is surviving this brutal punishment.

But after taking *stock* of your situation, you realize that this is . . .

THE END

Your hand trembles as you read the rest of the note.

If you can't rescue us, then hide the stones where the Lord High Executioner can never find them. We're sorry we got you into this. Good luck.

The note is signed "Edward and Susannah."

Find the stones? Rescue Eddie and Sue? From the Tower?

How do they expect you to do that? You don't even know where the Tower is.

Then you remember the note said something about a map. There's no map on the table.

You turn the note over and see a simple hand-drawn map on the back.

To check out the map, turn to PAGE 135. Then go to PAGE 128.

The king holds you in his piercing stare for what seems like an eternity. Then he glances away. You realize you were holding your breath.

"No, Sire," Lord Worcester replies. "Unfortunately, the prince and princess are still missing. But I shall not rest until I find them."

The king nods silently, then waves a hand to dismiss your master. You follow Lord Worcester as he backs away and joins the crowd of noblemen on one side of the great hall.

As you do, your eye catches a figure darting behind a purple curtain hanging on the sidewall. You can see that the curtain is hiding a door. It would be easy to slip through the crowd and disappear behind the curtain. This could be your chance to get away and explore the castle.

Still, Lord Worcester has been useful to you. He's gotten you this far. And he did say he was searching for Eddie and Sue. Maybe you should stick with him.

If you slip behind the curtain, go to PAGE 68.
If you stay in the Throne Room, go to PAGE 54.

You, Eddie, and Sue walk down the dimly lit tunnel. Minutes later, you come to a doorway. Eddie pushes it open, and the three of you walk into a small, windowless room.

"We're right behind the Throne Room," Sue whispers to you, pointing to a large wooden panel. She uncovers a peephole in the middle of the panel. You press your eye to it.

And almost cry out!

The king's throne is inches away. And beyond that is the vast Throne Room, crowded with richly dressed nobles.

Sue and Eddie kneel down next to you.

"We'll all push through at once," Sue whispers. "The person who ends up closest to the king should make a grab for the amulet."

You and Eddie nod.

"Ready?" Sue whispers. You nod again. She places her hands on the panel.

"Go!" she shouts, pushing it open.

And you all tumble into the Throne Room!

Land on PAGE 71.

"I'm game," you say. You pull the magic stone from your pocket and place it in the hollow in the box's lid.

Then you hold your breath.

A blue light and a small puff of smoke surround the box. As the smoke clears, you see the box is open. And lying inside it is a rolled-up parchment scroll.

You grab the scroll. Then you find the stone, which rolled onto the floor when the lid flew open.

"The scroll spell is designed for general use," the skeleton instructs you. "For best results, please use before May 15, 2001. Thank you for playing our game. You will now be returned to your previous location."

Before you can say a word, there's a flash of blinding white light. The next thing you know, you're standing back at the crossroads — in the exact place you were a couple of hours earlier.

In your hand is the scroll. Carefully you place it in your book bag.

Turn to PAGE 136 and write: Magic Scroll. Then turn to PAGE 32.

Eddie said it's the scepter, you think.

You leap forward and grab the heavy silver stick out of the king's hand. He stares in disbelief as you jump up and leap onto the bottom of the overturned throne.

"People!" you shout in your loudest voice. You wave the scepter at the crowd. "You're free! King Robert's evil rule is broken!"

Uh-oh. No one in the hall has moved. There's no wild cheering. No applause. Not even a tiny smile from anyone in the throng.

Then they all open their mouths and start shouting.

"Kill them! Kill the prince and princess and their evil friend!"

King Robert steps up to you and snatches back his scepter.

"The scepter is not the source of my power," he says quietly. He flashes you a wicked grin. "Nice try, though."

He turns to his soldiers.

"Take them to the Tower!" he commands.

This is it. You're about to be dragged to the Tower, where you'll have to face the Lord High Executioner. If only there was *someone* who would help you. But who?

_____

If you have the magic whistle, blow over to PAGE 126.

If you don't have it, turn to PAGE 79.

But you swing right by the balcony! Instead, you hurtle right through an open window. Your eyes are blinded by the sunshine. The rope reaches the end of its swing — and snaps!

You glance down as you seem to hang in the air for a moment, suspended above the castle's courtyard. Then you drop like a stone. You brace yourself for the sickening crash you'll feel when you hit the paving stones below.

But the shock never comes. You land with a thud in a pile of hay stacked in the back of a large oxcart. For a moment, you lie there with the wind knocked out of you. Then you grab handfuls of hay and cover yourself.

A few minutes later, you feel the cart start to roll. Yes! The cart has left the courtyard with you in it. You've escaped!

You lie in the hay as the cart moves slowly through the countryside. Later, when the castle is well behind you, you drop off the back.

As fast as you can, you make your way back to the crossroads.

First go to PAGE 136 and write down: Key to the Tower. Then turn to PAGE 32.

You have to help your friends!

You stumble toward the door, supporting yourself with one hand on the cool stone wall. In the doorway, you blink in the warm sunlight. You glance around. The hut is surrounded by well-kept fields of crops. Not far off you can see a thick forest. And running by the door is a dirt road.

Then you see what's making the noise — not to mention the stench. Standing in a small pen next to the hut is a fat, mud-covered hog!

Now you know what smells.

Then you hear another sound — like clanking metal. You turn. And gasp.

A pack of soldiers is running by! They're wearing armor and carrying swords, spears, and shields.

The lead soldier suddenly stops. He raises his iron-gloved fist — and points straight at you.

"You!" he cries in a thundering voice. "Surrender! In the name of the Lord High Executioner!"

Surrender? Yeah, right! Run as fast as you can to *PAGE 65.*

Eddie and Sue told me I'd feel weird, you think. I just didn't believe them.

You realize you'd better not touch the stones. Because — the thought hits you hard — you really are traveling in time!

You're shocked, scared, and amazed all at once. Then you don't feel or see anything.

The next thing you know, you're waking as if from a deep sleep.

You slowly open your eyes. You're lying on a lumpy, scratchy mattress. You guess it must be filled with straw. You glance up. The ceiling of the room is made of straw too.

The walls are stone. Pitchforks, a wooden rake, and a hoe hang from hooks. There's a fireplace, with a pile of peat stacked nearby. A rough wooden table, two chairs, and the bed you're lying on are the only other things in the room.

You take a deep breath. Sniff, sniff. What a stench! It smells like a barnyard in here!

"Sue and Eddie really did it," you marvel out loud. "I must be back in the Middle Ages." You glance around the hut again.

Hey! Where *are* Eddie and Sue? you think.

Search for them on PAGE 64.

You turn to Lord Worcester, trying to come up with an excuse for being where you are. But before you can utter a word, he raises a finger to his lips.

"Shh!" he whispers. "We don't want the Lord High Executioner to hear."

You stand there, stunned, as the nobleman slips through the curtain into the next room. He grabs the brass key from the table and holds it out to you.

"Here," he says in a low voice. "You'll need this."

You don't understand what's happening, but you do want the key. Haltingly you walk into the room and take it from him.

"Why?" you begin, but Worcester stops you again.

"Not here." He motions to a doorway — the same door that the Lord High Executioner went through. "Follow me."

Worcester steps through the doorway and waits for you to follow. "Quickly," he urges.

Your mind is reeling. Why is Worcester helping you? Or is he really leading you to the Lord High Executioner?

Do you dare trust him?

Turn to PAGE 136 and write down: Key to the Tower.

If you follow Worcester, go to PAGE 127.

If you don't follow him, go to PAGE 14.

You turn and see a ragged figure crouched against the wall. It uncurls itself and stumbles toward you.

It's a man. A very, very old man with long white hair and a beard. His matchstick-thin arms are bare, and he's wearing only a dirty rag around his body.

"Who are you?" you blurt out in fright.

"Who am I?" The man laughs, and you see he's missing all his teeth. He scratches his head. "Why, I can't seem to remember. It's been so long since I had someone to talk to! I'm glad they sent you down here to be with me."

"They didn't send me," you reply. "I fell while I was trying to get away from Lord Worcester."

"Lord Worcester?" The man looks at you. "He was dead long before they put me down here. You must have seen a ghost."

"No!" you shout. "He was just here. He must have come through a door or down a ladder."

"There's no way out," the man cackles. "It's a dungeon."

"No way out?" you repeat. "But —"

"Don't fret," he says. "They throw down food once a week."

"Once a week?" you moan as you sink to the floor.

"Oh, you get used to it after ten or fifteen years," he says cheerily. "Say, you didn't bring a deck of cards, did you?"

THE END

You can't hold your breath any longer. You have to get some air! Maybe you can swim to the bank before the creature recovers. You kick to the surface. Your head breaks into the sunlight, and your lungs fill with wonderful, fresh air.

But your moment in the sun doesn't last very long. Before you can take a second breath, cold tentacles grip your ankles.

"Help!" you shout to the guards who are watching from the drawbridge. But they just stare.

As the viselike grip on your ankles tightens, another coil reaches for your neck. You thrash in desperation, but there's nothing you can do. A second later you're pulled back under the dark, oozing crud.

This is the end, you think. You feel the breath being squeezed from your body. Thoughts of the magic stones, of Eddie and Sue, and of your home all flash through your mind. Then the creature pulls you down to the dark, watery bottom.

Wow, you realize. You don't even know *what* this creature is. But you're going to get the opportunity no modern scientist will get. You're going to study the creature!

From the inside out!

THE END

102

The three of you hit the throne hard.

The king gives a high-pitched shriek and leaps up. A dozen burly guards rush forward to protect him.

You have only seconds until they reach you. The king is just inches away. This is your only chance to grab the object that gives him his evil power!

But what is it? Your eye catches on an amber-colored amulet hanging from his neck. But then you remember what Eddie said about the scepter.

You only have a second.

Grab one!

If you grab the scepter, go to PAGE 95.
If you grab the amulet, go to PAGE 71.

You pull the soccer ball out of your book bag.

"This is one of our greatest inventions!" you declare. "In the future, all the kids play this game." You drop the ball and kick it away.

Your heart sinks as the ball travels through the air and hits one of Robin's men right in the head. But to your great relief, the crowd laughs.

"You aren't very good with that ball," Robin tells you. "Not for someone from the future."

She stares at you thoughtfully, raising one eyebrow. Then she says, "If you're such an expert at this game, prove it!"

"Prove it?" you echo nervously.

The outlaw leader puts two fingers in her mouth and whistles shrilly. Immediately, a dozen very large, muscular men form a tight line across the clearing.

"Get the ball past them," Robin says, "and we'll trust you. If you don't, we must banish you from this place."

You gaze down the clearing at the line of men. They're all over six feet tall, and their legs are like a line of tree trunks. Robin and the rest of her band watch expectantly.

Taking a deep breath, you drop the ball on the hard ground. You start to dribble toward the men.

Go to PAGE 72.

You stuff the three items into your book bag.

"Are you ready?" Eddie asks.

"Yup!" you reply. "Give me one of those rocks!"

"No!" Sue screams so loudly, you almost jump out of your seat. "The stones are dangerous," she adds gravely. "When the spell takes hold, you'll probably feel strange. But whatever happens, don't touch the stones. Is that clear?"

"Yeah, sure," you answer. This must be part of the trick.

"All right, Edward," Sue tells him. "You start."

Eddie places the first stone in his palm. Then he places the second and the third on top of it, till they form a small tower. You notice that the stones are glowing.

Cool! They're coated with glow-in-the-dark paint, you think.

Eddie begins to chant some corny spell.

"Movarum, Lovaris, Movarus!" he calls out.

Then the stones suddenly explode in a flash of blinding white light!

Blink and turn to PAGE 80.

You've been hanging out with Eddie and Sue a lot since they moved onto your block two months ago. They're cool. Sue is in sixth grade, with you. Her brother Eddie is in fifth. You would know if they were nuts. Wouldn't you?

"We aren't nuts," Sue says, almost as if she's reading your mind. "I know it's all hard to believe. But every word is true. And now we need your help."

"My help?" you say. "What for?"

"We have to go back to our time," Sue answers. "And we want you to come with us."

"Why do you have to go back?" you ask with a smirk.

"Because Morgred has used his wizard's power to look into the past," Eddie explains. "Uncle Robert is treating our subjects terribly. People are starving. Anyone who complains gets dragged away by the king's red-and-black-uniformed men . . . to the Tower."

Eddie shivers, and Sue squeezes his arm. She looks at you.

"We have to go back and free our subjects. We have to find a way to get King Robert off the throne. It's our royal duty."

"And we need someone else to help us," Eddie adds. "Someone the Lord High Executioner's men won't recognize."

"Someone," Sue says, "just like you."

Go to PAGE 76.

"No problem!" you tell Eddie and Sue. "I know where the king gets his power. He has an amber amulet — it's magic."

Eddie and Sue beam.

"I don't know how you learned that," Sue says. "But it's exactly what we needed to know if we're going to get Robert off the throne."

"Let's do it," Eddie says. "Let's go to the castle and face Uncle Robert."

Gulp. The thought of going to the castle makes you feel sick. But how else are you going to defeat the evil king?

The three of you slip out of the room and start down the stairs. But instead of going all the way to the bottom, Eddie stops halfway down. He pulls on the base of a torch holder on the wall. And a secret door slides open.

"Our father showed us this when he was still alive," Eddie explains. "It leads to the castle."

You peer into the long, dark tunnel.

And step through the door.

Go to PAGE 93.

You remember the magic scroll, the one you got in Morgred's Tower. You reach into your book bag and take it out.

The thin parchment glows brightly in the darkness. Carefully, you unroll it. The words on the scroll shine in silver letters.

With a trembling voice you say them out loud. "OUTRAY OUVRAY OPRAY!"

You hear a slight grinding noise, and some dust falls from the ceiling. Then slowly, haltingly, the door inches open. It stops after moving a foot, but there's enough room for you to squeeze inside.

You blink as your eyes adjust to the bright sunlight that's pouring through an open window. Then you spot the two figures who are staring at you in wonderment.

"Eddie! Sue!" you cry. "I found you!"

Go to PAGE 17.

108

These men are enemies of the king, you reason. So they must be good guys. Besides, they remind you of Robin Hood.

"I am pretty hungry," you declare. "Lead the way!"

"Excellent!" cries the leader. "One dinner, coming up!"

You follow them down a small path that leads away from the road. After being on your own in a strange place, it's nice to be with a bunch of friends. And they're all really careful to keep an eye on you and make sure you don't get lost.

After just a few minutes you see a low, rocky cliff. The path leads to a small cave that's partly hidden by vines. You follow the band into their hideout.

"Okay!" you shout, getting into the spirit of things. "What's for dinner?"

The leader turns to you with a big smile.

You stare at him. How come you didn't notice his teeth before? They're kind of — well, *pointy*.

"What's for dinner?" he repeats. "Funny you should ask."

Go to PAGE 114.

The key to Terror Tower! The Executioner might be keeping Eddie and Sue prisoner there now. If you want to rescue your friends, you're going to need that key.

The other man bows before the Executioner. Just then, you hear a third person enter the room from a door you can't see.

"Come quickly," the third voice orders. "The king awaits."

The two men hurry from the room.

Your heart leaps because you see what they have left behind, glinting in the candlelight.

The key to Terror Tower is on the table!

You can't believe your luck. All you have to do is rush out and grab it. You're just about to — when you hear a voice behind you.

"Wait!" someone whispers.

You turn and see Lord Worcester. He followed you into the chamber!

The key is right there. You might be able to grab it and get away — if you're fast enough. Or you might be able to persuade Worcester that you just got lost.

If you make a grab for the key, go to PAGE 50.
If you try to persuade Worcester you were lost, turn to PAGE 99.

110

The Executioner stares at Robert, who is struggling to get away from the people holding him.

Then he sees Eddie and Sue, surrounded by their subjects.

"You!" the Executioner thunders. "The prince and princess!" Then he bows low. "Welcome back, Your Highnesses."

The Executioner was under Robert's spell. And now he's free too!

The Throne Room erupts in cheers again.

"Long live Edward! Long live Susannah!"

That night, the celebrating goes on for a long time. But finally, after the feast is eaten and the candles have burned down, you and Eddie and Sue head up to the castle wing to their old bedrooms.

"Well, Your Majesties," you say. "Things turned out pretty well. I guess it's time for me to be getting back to my own time."

Sue gives you a sly look. "Your own time? I don't think so."

Go to PAGE 13.

There are too many guards at the front gate, you think. I'll try the smaller road. Maybe there are fewer guards.

You set off down the side road. You're alone on it. There are no crowds to hide in. The dark castle looms above you.

As you turn the corner of the castle, you see that the road leads to a smaller drawbridge, guarded by one soldier. His red-and-black tunic covers most of his brightly polished armor. In one hand he holds a round shield and in the other a long spear with a very sharp tip.

The guard stares at you with dark, beady eyes. In spite of your peasant clothing, you're sure he can tell you're a stranger. You have to drag your feet forward, fighting the urge to turn and run. The shadow of Terror Tower lies across your path like a dark pit. You step into it, and a chill flows through you.

At the start of the small drawbridge, your fear takes over. You freeze for a second. The guard scowls at you.

"Get on, then!" he barks. "They're waiting for you."

You don't have to be told twice. You don't know who's waiting, but it beats this scary guard. You walk quickly over the narrow bridge and through the arched stone doorway.

Go to PAGE 59.

"No, I don't, that is . . ."

It's all you can do to get out the words. Eddie and Sue look at you, and their faces drop.

"Then we're doomed," Sue says softly. "There's no way out of this room. I thought you had the other two stones and we could escape into the future with them. Now we're trapped here."

"And the Executioner —" you begin. But at that moment the heavy door bursts apart, split in two by a thick iron battering ram. The thin figure of the Lord High Executioner steps through the wreckage. He's followed by several soldiers. Their sharp swords gleam in the torchlight.

The Executioner's face is red with rage.

"You!" he shouts. "It was you who hurt me! But you'll pay for it now!"

You try to turn your head, but the Executioner glares at you with his red-rimmed, bloodshot eyes. You feel his gaze burning into your own eyes. The pain is intense — it feels as if white-hot pokers are being shoved into your eyes. You fall to the floor in a limp heap. You hear the Lord High Executioner laughing.

"Don't worry," he hisses. "That's just the beginning. You're going to be my guest for a long, long time."

THE END

He lowers you gently to the ground. When you stand up, you see five other men. They're dressed in green tunics and leggings. They carry long bows, and quivers of arrows, except for one very tall man who carries a long staff. That one is "Little" John. The man who spoke seems to be their leader.

"Sorry, traveler," he says now. "This trap was set for the king's soldiers, not a lone pilgrim like yourself."

"Uh, that's all right," you say awkwardly. You were frightened at first, but now this man seems kind and friendly. In fact, he reminds you of someone — but who?

Your thoughts are interrupted by the stranger.

"Say, we're just about to have our midday meal," he says, slapping you on the back. "It's only a modest repast, but we'd love to have you. What say you?"

These fellows could be just the help you need. Maybe you should go with them.

On the other hand, what do you really know about them, besides that they wear green tights?

If you go with the men, turn to PAGE 108.
If you'd rather be alone, turn to PAGE 52.

114

You suddenly start to feel nervous.

In the dim light of the cave, the band of men start to look fuzzy. Then, to your horror, they begin to change shape. As you watch, their leader's teeth grow longer and sharper, into deadly looking fangs. His back bends and twists, and his whole body swells and bulges horribly.

His face isn't pleasant and smiling anymore. Instead, he leers at you through bloodshot yellow eyes, like a dog's or a wolf's.

"Wh-wh-what are you?" you shriek. You turn in every direction, looking for a way out. It's no use. They have you surrounded.

"Why, we're ogres," the leader says with a cruel laugh. "What did you think? That we were some kind of merry men?"

"But you said —"

"I said we'd love to have you for dinner," the leader breaks in. He moves toward you, licking his lips. "And that's exactly what we're going to do."

THE END

I can't catch up, you think. I have to use the stones.

You kneel on the cold floor, cradling the three stones in your palm. Desperately, you try to remember the words Eddie used to make them work. With a trembling voice you cry:

"Movarum, Movoodoo, move over!"

There's a flash of blue light. Then your heart leaps for joy. You did it! In front of you is a group of people from your own time! They're wearing shorts, and colorful shirts, and wristwatches. Standing in front of them is a bald, red-faced man.

Then suddenly you realize you're still in Terror Tower! A dozen of the Executioner's soldiers are standing behind you. Instead of getting back to your own time, you've brought a group of people into the past. A group of tourists!

"Look, more actors," says a man in tan shorts and a red-and-blue-striped shirt. "Can we take a picture, Mr. Starkes?"

"Sure," says the bald man, who must be the leader. "Funny, I don't remember this exhibit. It must be new."

As the soldiers drag you away, you shout, "It's not an exhibit. It's real! Run for your lives!"

"Well, it must be new, Mr. Starkes," the man says. "Because these actors are terrible!"

THE END

116

You can't stand it anymore. You're going to suffocate.

You shoot out your fist and knock the stones from Eddie's hand. They fly into space. Then everything goes black.

Slowly, slowly you can breathe again. A soft blue light appears, covering everything. You feel yourself floating in a sea of fog. It's not hot, it's not cold, in fact it's like a lot of blue nothing.

"Hello!" you hear a faint voice. You can't tell if the person is miles away or right next to you.

"Why didn't you listen to me?" it says. "Why did you knock the stones away?"

"Eddie?" you say. It sounds as if you're talking underwater. "Where are we?"

"We're lost in time." That's Sue's voice. You can't even tell which direction it's coming from.

Fear grabs you like an icy hand.

"Get us out of here!" you cry.

"I can't," Eddie answers from far away. "The stones are gone. We're trapped here."

Turn to PAGE 8.

Nothing happens for a few minutes. The dragon sits there with your tape player in its ear. Then you see the great lizard's head begin to bob up and down in time with the music.

"Uh, dragon!" you murmur, trying to be polite. But it doesn't seem to hear you over the music from the earphones.

"Dragon!" you shout.

"Yes?" it answers, sounding a little annoyed.

"Uh, I was wondering," you say. "In this great treasure trove of yours, you wouldn't by any chance have any smooth white stones about so big?"

You hold your fingers apart to show him.

"White stones?" the dragon answers. "Hmm, yes, it seems to me I picked up one of those the other day. I think I left it in the back room. You can have it if you want."

"Thank you, mighty fire-breath!" you reply. You start to edge toward a hole in the back wall of the cavern.

"Don't mention it," the dragon tells you. Its head bops up and down. "But be careful," it adds. "After you get the stone, go up the shaft to the surface. Don't take any other tunnels."

"Thank you, oh broiler-mouth!" you cry. You turn and run for the back exit.

Go to PAGE 48.

118

It's a beautiful day in the countryside. The sky is bright blue, and a slight breeze blows across the fields.

You could almost forget that you've traveled eight hundred years back in time.

Then a picture of Sue and Eddie pops into your mind. You see them locked in a dark tower, chains on their feet and sharp blades hanging over their heads. You try to force the image away.

"First things first," you murmur to yourself. "I've got to find those stones. Then I'll think about how to rescue Eddie and Sue."

You take a deep breath and head down the road. Soon the road joins another one and becomes broader. With each step you feel fear and excitement growing in you. What will you see around the bend?

The road climbs a big hill. As you come to the crest you see a flat plain stretching for miles. Down below, several roads meet to form a crossroads. One of those roads leads to the Tower, you think. And you'll have to take it eventually.

With grim determination you start to walk down the other side of the hill.

Walk to PAGE 32.

Just then, something cold brushes against your leg. A fish? A plant? A ... *creature?*

Before you can swim a stroke, something rubbery wraps itself around one of your legs. Then it tugs you under!

You can't see anything in the blackness, but you feel more snakelike arms grabbing you, curling around your body, and pulling you to the bottom of the moat.

You struggle with all your might. You grasp a tentacle with both hands and pry it away from your neck. A second later, another tentacle wraps around your waist.

You're fighting for your life, and you're getting weak. Your arms are trapped at your sides now, but you keep kicking.

The creature's head must be below you. You aim your feet in that direction. With all the strength you have left, you strike out with your right foot. Your toes connect with something soft and fluid, like a large water balloon. Suddenly, all the strength goes out of the tentacles holding you. You slip free.

You realize you must have found the creature's weak spot. Did you kill it? Or is it only stunned? Should you try to swim away? Maybe you should try to kick it again.

If you swim for the surface, go to PAGE 101.
If you kick the creature again, go to PAGE 120.

120

I don't have a chance of outswimming this thing, you think. I just have to kick it in the same place again.

You turn and dive for the spot where you think the creature must be. Your hands plunge into something soft and mushy. Is it the creature's eye? Ick.

The creature seizes you around the chest with a tentacle that's as thick as a tree trunk. It swings you through the water. With a mixture of panic and relief, you realize it's trying to push you away.

You feel yourself sliding through the ooze. Suddenly, your head is above the water. But you're not in sunlight — it's pitch-black. You feel slimy stones under your hands and feet as you struggle out of the dank water.

Gasping and shivering, you lie there, breathing heavily until finally your lungs stop hurting.

Soon your eyes get used to the dark. The creature has thrown you into some sort of cave under the bank of the moat. A dim light shows you a tunnel leading away from the water. You have to follow the tunnel — because there is no way you're going back into the moat to face the creature again. You start crawling down the tunnel.

Crawl to PAGE 48.

You stand there, frozen to the spot. After what you just saw, you know you'll never get past those guards. But if you turn and walk away now, won't that make the guards suspicious? You're so scared, you nearly leap out of your skin when you feel a tap on your shoulder.

"Say there," says a friendly voice. "You wouldn't be looking for work, would you?"

You turn quickly, ready to run. But the man gazing down at you is smiling and friendly. He's tall and clean-shaven, with bright blue eyes. He has on a plumed hat, and his clothes are rich red-and-blue velvet. On his fingers he wears large jewels. You realize he must be a nobleman.

You're so tongue-tied, all you can do is stammer, "W-w-what?"

The man laughs. "I seem to have lost my page in the market, and I desperately need one before I present myself at court. Mustn't attend court without a page. I'll pay you, of course."

This could be your big chance. This nobleman can get you into the castle. But once you're inside, will you be able to get away from him? And what does a page do, anyway?

The seconds go by as he waits for your answer.

If you agree to be the nobleman's page, go to PAGE 24.

If you don't agree, go to PAGE 15.

You don't have time to waste eating lunch. You thank the stranger and stride off through the camp. It doesn't take long before you attract some attention.

"Hey!" A tall man with broad shoulders and thick, muscled arms approaches you. "What are ye doing in Robin's camp?"

A half dozen men and women gather behind him. Their faces are grim and angry.

"I'm looking for Robin," you reply.

"Are ye?" the man steps closer and squints at you. "And who be ye to look for Robin?"

"One of the king's spies!" someone in the crowd shouts. "Or from the Lord High Executioner!"

"But I'm not a spy!" You try to explain who you are, but your story is lost in the shouts from the crowd.

"Kill the spy!" someone screams. The tall man holds up his thick palm. "No, first we must have a trial," he says.

"Aye! A trial! Trial by combat!" The crowd roars.

Before you know it, you're being carried along by the crowd. They take you to a broad, fast-flowing stream crossed by a fallen tree trunk. The tall man hands you a thick staff. Then he jumps nimbly out onto the middle of the tree trunk.

You have a sinking feeling you know what's coming next.

Go to PAGE 58.

Who knows? Maybe the Tower door isn't even locked. You reach for the doorknob.

Before you can touch it, a blue spark jumps from the iron knob to your hand.

"Yeow!" You draw your hand back, rubbing your fingers in pain. You gaze at them, but they don't seem to be burned. And the pain quickly fades.

It takes you a few seconds to realize that all the feeling in your hand is fading.

You peer at your hand again. In horror, you see that your fingers have turned gray and hard, almost like — stone!

Suddenly the truth hits you. Those stone statues aren't statues at all — they're people the Lord High Executioner has turned into stone. And now his magic is doing the same to you.

In panic, you turn to run, but your feet are frozen to the ground. You look down and see that they've already turned to cold, gray granite. In just a few seconds all of you will be transformed. You'll be stuck, standing by the road and guarding Terror Tower for all eternity.

As the gray numbness spreads through your body, you can't help thinking, Standing for all eternity? Why didn't I at least sit down first?

THE END

Feeling defeated, cold, and tired, you turn around to walk back down the stairs. But before you can take a single step, you see candlelight. And then you hear a voice that chills you.

"Who dares enter my tower? Who dares enter the realm of the Lord High Executioner?"

You try to answer, but instead you fall to your knees in fear and tumble down the cold, hard stairs.

You must have blacked out, because when you awake, you are in a dark, foul-smelling place, up to your waist in mud and ooze. Heavy chains are locked around your wrists. And a shovel is in your hands.

"Get to work, slave!" growls a menacing voice. Standing above you on a rock is a brute of a man, dressed in long black robes. He holds an evil-looking whip.

"You're a slave of the Lord High Executioner now," he says.

In the gloom you see other figures, chained like you, shoveling the mud. You turn to the man next to you.

"What are we shoveling?" you ask.

"Don't know," he grunts with a toothless mouth.

"Silence!" the overseer barks. The cruel whip lashes out. But the pain you feel is nothing compared to the pain of knowing you're doomed to stay there — forever.

THE END

"Okay," you nod to the boy. "I'll go with you."

The grimy boy grins. He pulls you down a narrow dirt lane. Soon you come to a tumbledown cottage surrounded by a muddy yard.

"Hey, Da!" the boy shouts. Immediately a tall, very strong-looking man stoops under the low doorway. His bald head glints in the sun, and his narrow brown eyes stare at you in puzzlement.

"Who's this?" he growls at the boy.

"Someone who *wants* to do homework!" the boy exclaims.

The boy's father turns his heavy pink face toward you. "*Like* homework, do ye?" he says with an evil grin.

You suddenly realize that people in the Middle Ages have a different idea about homework. In a flash, the big man lunges at you and seizes your shoulders in a painful iron grip.

"We gots plenty of homework here," he says. He points to a hoe lying in the mud. "Pick it up!" he shouts. "Do your homework. And don't try to sneak off!"

You stare at the large, muddy field. You can't believe it. You traveled all the way to the Middle Ages to wind up working as a field hand!

You struggle to lift the hoe. As you do, you have a shocking thought. For the first time in your life, you wish you *were* doing homework!

THE END

126

The magic whistle! you think. The one that Robin gave me!

You grab it from your pocket and hold it to your lips. You get out one short blast — then a soldier snatches it from your lips.

The sweet, clear note hangs in the air for a long moment.

"Thank you for the music." King Robert sneers. "But we don't have time for a concert. However, you will sing for the Lord High Executioner. Sing in pain, that is."

You look at Eddie and Sue and see that they're shivering.

"Before you go to the Tower," the king continues, "you will be paraded through the village. Let the people see how useless it is to resist my will!"

You, Sue, and Eddie are hauled away by soldiers, out of the Throne Room and into the large courtyard. The three of you are tossed into the back of a wagon and surrounded by mounted guards.

"There must be a hundred of them," Sue says as the procession rolls out of the courtyard and down the wide road leading from the castle.

"We'll never get out now," Eddie moans.

"I guess not," you say.

Roll to PAGE 5.

You don't know why, but Worcester seems to be on your side. After all, he just gave you the key to the Tower. And if he wanted to turn you in, all he had to do was yell for the guards.

You decide to trust him. You follow him through the door, ready to run at the first sign of the Executioner.

Just on the other side of the doorway, Worcester stops. He pushes against a solid-looking wood panel. The wall slides back easily, revealing a narrow shaft and a ladder leading down. He swings onto the ladder and motions for you to follow.

Your hands grip the ladder rungs tightly as you climb down into the darkness. Then the wooden wall slides back into place with a snap. The shaft is pitch-black! You have to feel with your feet for every rung. Finally you reach the bottom and find yourself in a low, stone tunnel, lit by sputtering torches.

"What is this place?" you ask jokingly. "The dungeon?"

"Yes, it is," Lord Worcester replies with a thin smile. "And it's also my home."

Go to PAGE 77.

128

You carefully fold the map and put it in your book bag.

You peek out the doorway of the hut. You are surrounded by fields. Right in front of the door is a dirt road that leads into a thick cluster of trees. How are you supposed to know where to go?

This is too scary! You wish you could get back to your own time and your own house. You wish this was a dream. But you know it's not.

How are you supposed to find the stones? And how can Eddie and Sue expect you to sneak into the Tower and save them? It's impossible!

Then you notice something that cheers you up a little. Hanging on a peg behind the door are some simple woolen clothes. At least you'll blend in with the people here.

You take off your jeans and T-shirt and slip on the woolen garments. They're scratchy and they don't smell great. But they'll do. There's a pair of leather boots. You pull them on. They're surprisingly comfortable. Suddenly you don't feel quite so afraid.

You pick up your book bag and step out the door into the warm sunshine.

Step to PAGE 118.

"We have to prepare first," Sue replies. "There's a limit to how much the stones can transport. You can only take three things with you."

"Three things?" you repeat. "Like what?"

"Anything that might come in handy in a fight," Eddie suggests.

"Or that might get the people to follow us — and help us overthrow King Robert," Sue adds.

Your beat-up green book bag is lying on the floor next to your soccer ball. You unzip the bag and dump out its contents. Besides a couple of school textbooks and half a peanut butter sandwich, this is what you see:

> a pocket flashlight
> a tape player
> a pair of sunglasses
> a soccer ball

What would you bring if you really were going back in time? you ask yourself.

Flash light
Sunglasses
Soccer ball

Choose three items. Turn to PAGE 136 and write down the three things you would take. Then turn to PAGE 104.

This road must lead to a village, you think. It might even be the village where Eddie and Sue went for supplies.

You stride down the narrow dirt road. Then you hear noises from behind — men shouting, metal clanging on metal, horses neighing.

You don't know who is coming, but you want to be able to see them before they see you. Quickly, you haul yourself out of the mud and scramble onto the high, grassy shoulder of the road. You crouch behind a few scraggly bushes.

You're just in time. A troop of heavily armored knights appears around a bend. Each knight wears a red-and-black tunic over his armor and each carries a long, sharp lance pointed skyward. Long red-and-black flags flap in the wind.

Red and black, you think. Why does that ring a bell? Then you remember — Eddie and Sue told you that red and black are King Robert's colors. Those must be his soldiers.

The earth trembles as the horses storm by. When they have disappeared, you walk back onto the road. The soldiers went in the same direction you were heading. Do you follow?

If you follow, turn to PAGE 42.
Or return to the crossroads on PAGE 32.

"They'll know you're a stranger!" the girl whispers. "Get out of here — now!"

You hear the sound of heavy footsteps moving from door to door in the village.

The girl suddenly turns and dashes out of the square, leaving you alone. You start to follow her when the door to the nearest cottage pops open. A round-faced woman with long red hair pokes her head out.

"Here, you!" she calls softly. "Ye don't want to be seen by them, do ye? Get inside and I'll hide ye!"

The woman's face is worried. She motions to you with a plump hand. You hear the soldiers getting closer. Any minute they'll come around the corner. You don't know if you can outrun them. But can you trust this woman?

If you trust her, turn to PAGE 73.
If you run away, turn to PAGE 27.

You follow your new master through giant doors leading into a huge hall. He directs you to a small side room. There he orders you to change from your peasant's clothing into the blue velvet garments of a nobleman's page. Then you and your master step into a big room with a throne at one end.

From somewhere a servant calls out, "Lord Worcester!"

You realize that's your master's name.

He sweeps grandly down the long aisle. On either side are more noblemen and women. You try to keep yourself from shaking in fear as you follow him. But this is a nightmare. You're walking straight toward your friends' greatest enemy!

Lord Worcester stops ten feet in front of the throne and bows. You realize you should bow too.

The king has a thick beard and curly black hair that hangs down to his shoulders. He has a very unpleasant look on his face, as if he's just eaten something rotten.

"Lord Worcester," the king says, "any word of my dear niece and nephew? I am *so* worried about them."

You feel as if you're going to faint. The king is talking to Lord Worcester — but he's staring right at *you*!

Try not to faint as you turn to PAGE 92.

"Well, it does say it's for emergencies," you tell yourself as you turn to page 2001. The instructions on the parchment page are very short.

IN CASE OF EMERGENCY, REPEAT THESE WORDS THREE TIMES: ESS OH ESS NYNE WON WON.

That's all? you wonder. Then you take a deep breath and follow the instructions.

When you're done, you brace yourself for something terrible — or wonderful. But you jump in fright when the skeleton in the corner begins to talk.

"Attention!" it says. "You are an unauthorized spell maker. You will be removed from the premises."

Before you can say anything, there's a flash of blinding white light. The next thing you know, you're standing back at the crossroads in the exact place you were a couple of hours earlier.

"It was a magic burglar alarm!" you mutter.

You take a moment and catch your breath. As far as you can tell, you're still in one piece.

Well, you think. I'm back where I started. But at least I didn't turn myself into a frog or something.

From out of nowhere, you hear the voice of the skeleton.

"Not this time."

Go to PAGE 32.

134

You place your hands on the door and give it a push. It's as solid as the stone walls around it.

Taking a deep breath, you bang your fist on the door.

BOOM!

The whole tower vibrates like a huge drum. You have to hold your ears until the sound dies down. But when it does, there's still no sign of life anywhere.

I guess no one is home, you think. You glance up. And see some letters carved in the stone just above the doorway.

KMPEPCB + 2

Maybe it's a password, you think. Maybe if I say those letters, the door will swing open.

You take a closer look at the jagged rocks around the door — the ones that look like teeth. Maybe the door won't swing open. Maybe something terrible will happen! Maybe you should study the letters a little longer and see if you get a brilliant idea.

If you say the letters, go to PAGE 18.
If you study them longer, turn to PAGE 31.

THE MAP

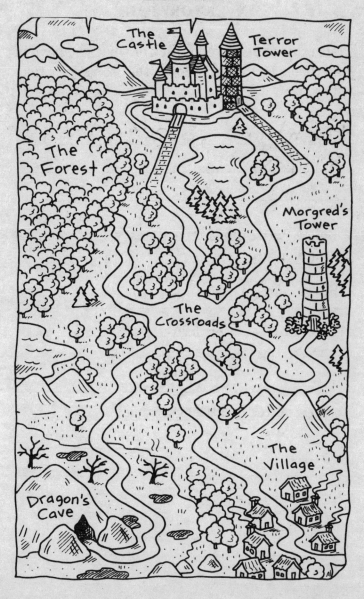

136

INVENTORY PAGE

Use this page to keep track of what you have in
your book bag. Write down the items you take
with you:

Flashlight , soccer ball,
sunglasses

Below, write down the items you pick up on
your adventure:

Key to the tower
magic scroll
magic stone
magic wistle
magic stone

About R.L. Stine

R.L. Stine is the most popular author in America. He is the creator of the *Goosebumps, Give Yourself Goosebumps, Fear Street,* and *Ghosts of Fear Street* series, among other popular books. He has written nearly 200 scary novels for kids. Bob lives in New York City with his wife, Jane, teenage son, Matt, and dog, Nadine.

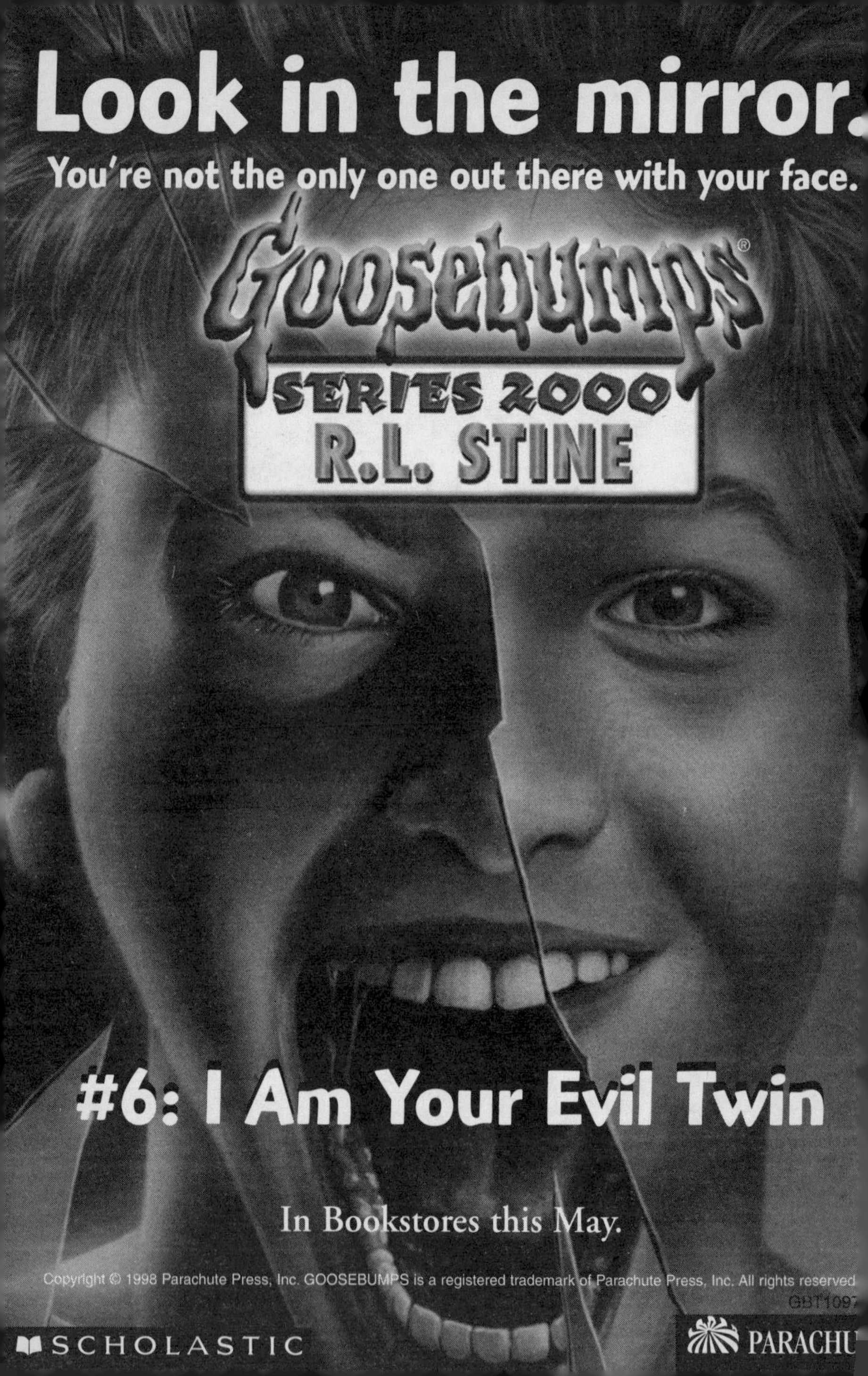
Look in the mirror.
You're not the only one out there with your face.
Goosebumps®
SERIES 2000
R.L. STINE
#6: I Am Your Evil Twin
In Bookstores this May.
Copyright © 1998 Parachute Press, Inc. GOOSEBUMPS is a registered trademark of Parachute Press, Inc. All rights reserved.
GBT1097
SCHOLASTIC
PARACHU

Feeling Clawstrophobic?

GIVE YOURSELF

Danger at Every Turn!

Goosebumps®

R.L. STINE

Choose Wisely!

You're spending the summer in a house on Cat Cay Island. The caretaker warns you not to go outside after dark. But when your brother disappears, you have no choice.

Want to check the old lighthouse? Watch your step—it's one big booby trap. Prefer the caretaker's cottage? Beware of the Cat Woman. She's looking for someone to take her place—and she's got her eye on you!

Give Yourself Goosebumps #28:

Night of a Thousand Claws

Visit the Web site at http://www.scholastic.com/goosebumps

Get scratched at a bookstore near you!

SCHOLASTIC   PARACHUTE